Orion's Daughters

ORION'S DAUGHTERS

a novel

Courtney Elizabeth Mauk

Engine Books
Indianapolis

Engine Books
PO Box 44167
Indianapolis, IN 46244
enginebooks.org

Printed in the United States of America

10   9   8   7   6   5   4   3   2   1

ISBN: 978-1-938126-94-9

Library of Congress Control Number: 2014935028

For Eric

Pledged to the spirit alone, the founders anticipate no hasty or numerous addition to their numbers. The kingdom of peace is entered only through the gates of self-denial; and felicity is the test and the reward of loyalty to the unswerving law of Love.

—Louisa May Alcott, "Transcendental Wild Oats"

Spring

one

FROM THE TIME WE were small, Amelia had a knack for storytelling. She could string words together like the pastel candies on the necklace she wore as a bracelet, twisted four times around her skinny wrist. Like those candies, her words never split or cracked, they never fell off into the grass and were lost. I did not have her skill. Two days after her grandfather gave us those necklaces mine had been destroyed by my sweet tooth and my carelessness. My natural role was second best, Amelia's listener. She liked to tease me. "Now you go," she'd say, breaking off at a pivotal moment—the children just captured by the goblin beneath the porch, the defenseless woman just cornered by the serial killer in the woods—and I would startle, gaping and gasping, language lost to me completely.

She would smile, wrap her hands around a tree limb, and hoist herself into the air, grass-speckled toes swinging next to my face.

"Never mind," she'd say. "I'll tell you."

Only when she resumed her telling could I relax. As she spoke, my mind opened wide, ready to receive. I lived for her stories.

That is to say, I lived inside her stories.

But I don't anymore. I haven't for a very long time.

Tension extends from my chest, out through my arm, and into my fingers as I scrape at the postcard taped to my front door.

The image is familiar: a dense forest in spring green, *Cuyahoga Valley National Park* in stylized white cursive in the upper left hand corner. Below the canopy I imagine our cabins, the doors open and rooms freshly swept, empty and awaiting our return. But that's impossible. The cabins would be filled with other voices, other bodies, other smells, echoes of our own.

Before, the postcards always arrived by mail. I look over my shoulder. The front yard is empty. No cars pass. Has it been hours, or minutes, since Amelia stood in this exact spot?

Stepping back, I try to see my house through her eyes. Last week, at Maya's urging, I hung a wreath on the door. It's a cheap thing: plastic flowers and pink and yellow ribbons, a little wooden rabbit, a sign that says *Hoppy Easter*. I look at this silly decoration, the white aluminum siding, the fake green shutters, the picture window—everything that belongs to me—the way Amelia would see it and the tension in my chest slams into the pit of my stomach.

In the driveway my car sits with the door open. I abandoned it as soon as I saw the glint of the postcard on my door, but now I leave the card where it is and go back. My high heels sink into the grass; Peter mowed yesterday, and blades cling to the feet of my pantyhose. As I start the car, I glance over at the manila folder on the passenger seat, the contract revisions my boss wants me to look over before tomorrow morning's meeting. In half an hour I have to pick Maya up from school. I have dinner to cook, her homework to oversee, mine to start. I don't have time for Amelia's nonsense, not today, not in this life.

I pull into the garage, go into the house, dump my purse and folder on the kitchen table. I manage to pour a glass of orange juice before I open the front door, strip off the tape, hold the postcard in my hand.

I turn it over, expecting nothing. She has never written a message before, not even a return address. But there, taped to the blank white space, is a folded piece of notebook paper.

Breathing deeply from my diaphragm, the way Amelia and I were taught, I pull the notebook paper free.

Sara
355 Harper Ave, Apt. 2B
Chicago

All right, Amelia. All right.

I take the postcard and scrap of paper upstairs to our bedroom and settle into the meditation area below the window, on top of the yoga mat, among the purple and blue silk pillows that still smell of the store's Nag Champa incense, with the late afternoon sunlight warm against my back. Sitting cross-legged, my shins no longer run parallel, my knees no longer touch the floor. Regardless, I am better at meditating now than I was as a child. I no longer grow bored. I don't make up songs in my head or slit my eyes to sneak glances around the room. With age I've learned to hold still and concentrate on my breathing. I can inhale, exhale, and let go.

In the space beside me, I feel Amelia's heat, the rise and fall of her breath synchronized with mine.

My eyes pop open.

Our unmade bed. And underneath: a litter of dust bunnies, too many dropped tissues to count, a pair of sandals, and wadded up in the corner, one of Peter's rarely worn ties. Red and blue stripes.

Sara.

I roll the name around my mouth like a pebble.

Sar-a.

Above the house Amelia circles—a hawk sensing my weakened state. My skin prickles with anticipation of the shrill call, the knock on the door.

two

Sara was supposed to be Maya's name. As eight year olds, Amelia and I both vowed to name a daughter after Amelia's mother. But when I gave birth ten years ago, I chose Maya. The decision felt liberating. Peter—inventive, always aware of impressions—told our family and friends that we chose the name because the Maya civilization had been the first to develop a fully written language; our daughter likewise embodied the dawning of a new era. We are a smart, cultivated family. Truthfully, I chose the name for its possessiveness—My-a. Mine.

People are always telling me that Maya is a beautiful name.

My daughter doesn't know about my childhood, about Amelia. Not in detail. As she's gotten older, she's become curious and I have intended to tell her the truth. At night, propped up against her pillow, I've brushed back her hair. I've made my voice light.

I've said, "Once upon a time, there were two little girls."

I've said, "They were the only two children in the world."

That's when I lose my nerve. She looks up at me with wide child-eyes, hazel, like Peter's, and my tongue affixes to the roof of my mouth.

I end up telling her about Snow White or Hansel and Gretel, stories whose consequences are certain, their safety known.

✳

If I were braver, I would tell my daughter this:

Amelia lived with her grandfather, Robert, across the pond from my family's cabin. The pond was man-made, dug out of the Ohio clay by Tammy and Steve O'Sullivan, the founders of Orion Community, and meant to be a point of beauty and relaxation. Instead mud clouded the water, the air above swarming with mosquitoes in summer. When we swam, we emerged dirtier than when we entered, our feet cut by rocks. Amelia loved the pond anyway. While I treaded water near the shore, she'd take a deep breath and dive underneath, reappearing on the other side with her hair plastered over her face and her eyes as red as if she'd been crying. She told me about the things she saw below: an unlaced boot caught by its toe between two rocks; a pearl necklace minus its pearls; a naked Barbie doll submerged from the waist down in the mud, her arms raised as if asking for help.

My family joined Orion when I was five. Amelia had been there since she was a few months old; as the only child, Orion was hers. Tammy rocked her to sleep, held her hands when she took her first steps. If she could have, I'm sure Tammy would have suckled Amelia at her breast.

My coming had been presented to Amelia as a gift: here is your friend, your sister. As if Tammy had carried me in her womb, as if she had molded me out of the Ohio clay, so Amelia would not have to be alone anymore.

Here she is. Just for you. Take her.

From her side of the water Amelia watched Robert help my father build our cabin. She saw the walls go up, the roof take shape. She saw their arms flailing hammers, their knees bending as they hoisted planks of wood, their skin turning pink and then red and then brown in the sun. She heard their exhalations, their curses, their laughter. At the end of the day, when my father came over to drink apple cider on her porch, she smelled their sweat and felt their tired, heavy hands smooth down her hair. When she told me these things, I felt a jealousy so intense, it burned beneath my ribs for hours, flaring up again at night as I stared up at the ceiling my father had built and tried to picture him as she had described: strong, competent, male.

Amelia waited on our steps the morning my father drove my mother and me through the Orion gates; past long, low Home, the only building with running water or electricity, where we would attend meetings and eat most of our meals; and along the rutted path past the five other cabins to our allotment at the back of the ten-acre property. I'd been told a little girl my age lived here, but the sight of her shocked me. Her physical presence made everything real, and I wanted my father to turn the car around and take us back through the gates, down the highway to our comfortable house, our normal life. But it was too late. We had already sold everything that wasn't in the back of the station wagon, and my parents were kissing, my mom's back pressed against the dashboard, my dad's hand up the front of her Indian print shirt, revealing her pale, puckered stomach.

I slipped out of the car and approached Amelia, who watched with an expression of calm detachment, a look I would later think of as her robot face. She wore denim shorts and a white tank top, her blond hair in a sloppy ponytail, her feet bare and dirty. The cabin seemed to be her home, not mine.

I stopped at the base of the steps. "I'm Carrie," I said, as if my name could assert ownership.

"You took a long time," she said.

"Only half an hour."

"All summer. It's August now."

She took my hand and led me away from my parents.

The grass around the pond grew long and wild, making me think of the watering holes in Africa on the nature shows my dad and I liked to watch. I wished we could watch one now, but the television had been sold and I wasn't supposed to call them Mom and Dad anymore. They were Glory and Mike. They'd made me practice all spring and summer, but the names still felt foreign, their use forced.

When we reached Amelia's cabin, she stopped and batted my hand away.

"Do you know your history?" she said.

I stared at this strange girl, the cabin looming up behind her, identical to our cabin across the water.

"There were the pilgrims," I said slowly. "They came in the Mayflower."

"No." She ground her fists into her skinny hips and pointed her toe, tapping the ground with each word like a teacher hitting a ruler against a blackboard. "Our history. The community's."

Behind me came the sound of my parents' laughter, the doors of the station wagon banging shut. Amelia pointed to my necklace, a gold heart pendant Glory had given me for Valentine's Day the year before.

"That isn't yours," she said.

I slapped my hand over the necklace, but I landed wrong, digging the point of the heart into my chest.

"Yes, it is," I said.

"Here we share everything. It's all communal." She paused. "Do you know what that means? There's no difference between yours and mine, or you and me. We're all the same. The children and the adults."

"We're not the same," I said, "and it's my necklace."

"If you're not going to follow the rules, you can't live here. Larry and Justine and Samantha Carbuncle, they didn't follow the rules and they had to leave. They were selfish, and they were materialistic. They stole money from the safe box in Home. Stealing is especially bad here."

Beside the pond, the sun glared down on me with nothing to block it, and I felt captured, exposed. I wasn't stealing; the necklace was mine fair and square. Glory had given it to me, but what would she want me to do now? Over the last few weeks she'd lectured me on the importance of sharing, of giving back to the world, although she had never explained how or exactly why. I couldn't be sure of the rules anymore.

I didn't look at Amelia as I took the necklace off.

She laughed. "I don't want to wear it, silly."

My hand hovered in the space between us, the necklace draped across my palm.

"Why are you being mean?" I said.

"I'm not mean." She grabbed my hand, locking the necklace between her skin and mine. "I'm teaching you."

✳

HERE IS THE FIRST story Amelia told me, my new history:

Tammy and Steve O'Sullivan wanted a child more than anything else, but for years they tried and failed to have one. When Tammy turned forty, they stopped trying, and a month later they conceived their son Orion. A miracle.

Just after his third birthday, Orion became ill. The doctors ran test after test but could find nothing wrong. That's when Tammy realized the danger resided not within Orion's body but without. She threw away all her cleaning products, rid the house of man-made fibers, switched the family to an organic vegan diet, but the changes came too late. Orion grew worse. He died within a year.

Unable to live within the society that had killed their son, Tammy and Steve moved to land inherited from Tammy's grandfather and built their own cabin from trees they felled, planted a garden that would provide their food. Yet despite their hard work, they still felt empty. To search their souls, they went on a month-long cleanse, drinking only water and apple cider and not speaking. By the end their bodies were near death but their minds never more alive. They realized they acted selfishly keeping this pure way of life a secret. They needed to invite others to join them so that the movement would grow and change society for good.

Robert and Amelia had been the first family to join Orion. They were brave pioneers, part of a revolution. Few who came lasted longer than six months. The evils of SAS (Standard American Society) were difficult to forsake after whole lives of indoctrination. Even Steve had given in to temptation and left two years before my family arrived.

"We don't like tourists," Amelia said. "We can spot who they are real quick."

"Am I a tourist?" I asked.

"No." She grinned. "You're mine."

I was just beginning to understand the power of her words. Like a magic wand waved above my head, turning me into something new.

three

I AM FIFTEEN MINUTES late picking Maya up from school. Behind the chain link fence, she runs, unzipped jacket flapping, reaching out to tap another girl's arm. They are playing tag, six of them, scuffed tennis shoes pounding, faces flushed. The mothers watch from the sidewalk. Every pick up I tell myself that I will join them, and once in a while, when I'm in an especially good mood, I do. Today I don't even pretend. I know I am not budging from this car.

The postcard is on the dashboard, the trees reflected spectrally in the windshield; Sara's address I've stowed away in my wallet, tucked behind Maya's school picture. I resist the urge to check the back of the postcard again for the words that aren't there, the missing answers to my questions: Where are you? Why now? What do you want from me?

What do I have left to give you?

I lay my elbow on the horn.

The mothers turn. Maya freezes, foot lifted mid-run, and looks at me in irritation. One of the mothers—Shirley, I think, yes, Shirley Benson, Isabella's mom—waves at me. I wave back.

Shirley approaches. With no choice, I roll my window down.

"Hi, Carrie," she says, leaning inside, her perfume an overwhelming citrus. "How are you?"

"Good," I say. She doesn't seem to notice the postcard, but I wish I'd had time to remove it from the dashboard, place it on the seat beside me, cover it with my hand.

"As you know," Shirley says, "I'm room mother this year."

I didn't know—or I'd forgotten—but I do know what's coming next: my delinquency.

"We're making the list for the end-of-year party," she says. "Can I put you down for some summery treats?"

On the playground Maya hugs each one of her friends, moving down the row like a guest on a receiving line.

"Okay," I say. "Sure."

"Great! What'll it be? Don't feel like you have to bake something. We always need soda or napkins. Paper plates are fantastic."

Paper plates: the desperate mother's contribution. I press my feet against the floor and stretch my body up so that I'm sitting erect and alert. I look straight at Shirley. "Lemon bars," I say. "I have a great vegan recipe. Maya loves them."

I don't know why I lie. Maya hates when I cook vegan.

"Oh, right. You're one of those 'healthy moms.' Good for you! I wish I could do it. I have the best intentions, you know, but they love their chips and Fruit Roll-Ups!"

"I'm not always healthy," I say, thinking of the Oreos I packed in Maya's lunch. Peter is the one to pack healthy meals, but he's been teaching an early class this semester, putting in long hours at the lab. The mornings are my responsibility, and I've never been a morning person.

"I'll put you down for those lemon bars," Shirley says. "They sound absolutely yum!"

As she turns away, I roll up my window fast.

Maya climbs in the back.

"Good day at school?" I ask.

"It was all right." She unzips her book bag and takes out a folder. The cover is a shimmery metallic and in different light looks purple or pink or silver.

"Any homework?"

"Math and reading."

"What's the math?"

"Geometry."

"Oh, I never was very good at that."

She searches through her bag, coming up with a pencil. "I'm good," she says.

I switch on the radio. A man with a booming voice shouts about a sale on Toyotas. I change the channel—an R&B song with a nice beat, but I can't be sure the lyrics are appropriate. I scan until I get to NPR. The safe, golden chords of a harp.

Maya draws her knees to her chest and begins biting her thumbnail.

"Don't do that," I say.

She ignores me; I should let such a small infraction go, but I can't.

"Mi amour," I say. "Get your finger out of your mouth and put your feet on the floor."

She flops back, extending her legs, flinging her hands to her sides. "Why?" she says, the syllable drawing out.

"Well, for one thing, your fingers are dirty. And for another, if I make a sudden stop, you'll knee yourself in the throat. You'll get hurt."

Her eyes roll up to the ceiling and don't come back down.

I can't stand when she's mad at me. Lately Peter and I have been arguing too often, too loudly, forgetting she's within hearing range, or even in the same room. It's shameful—I swore I wouldn't recommit the sins of my parents. But my daughter is resilient, just like Amelia. When Amelia fell out of a tree, she would roll on to her side and hold still for just a second before getting up, wiping off her jeans, and climbing again. She never cried. When we found a dead bird or squirrel in the woods, she would prod it with a stick. "Natural causes," she'd say. Or, "Must have been a dog or cat." She'd toss the stick aside and continue on while I fought the urge to touch the feathers, the matted fur, to grieve for something I didn't understand but knew had to do with me, with her, with Glory and Mike, Robert and Sara.

I envy resilience. I have always been too soft, too emotional, too dependent on the resilience of others. I am glad my daughter is not like me. She is more like Peter: solid, stoic.

She takes her math book from her bag and begins working her problems.

"I heard from a friend today," I say, but Maya is concentrating on her homework.

✳

Amelia pointed to the shelf just inside her cabin's door. "My mother's shrine," she said.

In the dim light I could make out the silver frame, the white votive candles on either side, the dried roses tied with a pink ribbon.

Amelia dragged over a chair and climbed on top to reach the photograph. We took it out to the porch for better light. The woman was young, a teenager really, with Amelia's wispy blond hair. She sat on the steps of a blue house and faced the camera with a small smile, hard eyes, as if daring the lens to contradict her.

"Where is she?" I asked.

"Dead."

I looked at Amelia, trying to decide if she was joking, if this was a trick like the necklace.

"What do you mean?"

"I mean she's dead. Robert scattered her ashes in the field next to their old house. She liked to play there when she was our age. He told me flowers bloomed. All sorts of flowers, all colors of the rainbow. They'd never grown there before."

"How?"

"She made them grow."

"No. How did she die?"

"Childbirth."

I didn't understand: childbirth didn't lead to death. Childbirth was happy. When Glory saw a pregnant woman at the grocery store, she smiled and asked when the baby was due, even though she didn't like to talk to strangers. Sometimes she even touched the woman's belly. No one seemed afraid.

"Bleeding," Amelia said. "She died giving me life. There is no greater sacrifice."

She kissed the photograph and held it out to me. When I didn't move, she shook the frame until I took it from her and kissed the smeared glass, right where her lips had been.

Through the pond grasses, I spotted Glory's dark hair as she moved back and forth from the station wagon to the cabin. Until that moment, I had never considered that she could die. Bleed to death.

We had been at Orion for less than an hour.

"Hush." Amelia brought her face close to mine. "Don't cry."

"I'm not."

She hugged Sara's picture to her chest and watched as I tried to suck the tears back in.

✳

I DON'T KNOW HOW I got onto the highway, but here I am, speeding along, keeping up with traffic as if I belong. Maya hasn't noticed. She keeps her head bent over her homework.

I turn the radio up.

My false move.

"Mom. Where are we going?"

"Just a little detour, mi amour."

"It's a school night."

"Live a little."

I take my eyes from the rearview mirror and focus on the road. The hills have increased, the trees growing thicker. Up ahead I see the green exit sign: Cuyahoga Valley National Park.

"My stomach hurts," Maya says.

I ease up on the gas and open the glove compartment, remove a roll of Dramamine, toss it in the back.

"I need something to drink," Maya says.

"They're the chewable kind."

I turn the music all the way up. A tango ricochets off the walls of the car. Maya covers her ears with her hands.

✳

"FROM SUCH AUSPICIOUS BEGINNINGS," Amelia said. I asked what auspicious meant. "The best of the best of the best."

We made Sara our own Snow White, our own Sleeping Beauty.

In the grass Amelia lay with her hair fanned out, her arms crossed over her chest, her eyes closed.

I dropped to my knees beside her and picked up her hand. Her wrist hung limp. I let the hand fall, smack against the other.

Her face, too still. A doll's face. A death mask.

I pretended to forget my lines so she would wince.

"Please no," I said.

A deeper frown. I pressed my ear to her chest in what I hoped was a sufficiently desperate manner.

I heard nothing. She was too good at this game. I could imagine her lying in the grass as day turned to night, as the seasons changed, freezing and thawing, weeds growing up between her fingers and toes, birds tearing at her hair, carrying away golden strands for their nests.

"Sara." I tilted my chin toward the sky and yelled with everything I had. "Don't leave me here!"

The trees sent my voice back.

My tears came again, only this time I knew the tears were right, they were justified.

I kissed her forehead.

All the fairytales had promised that this would be the remedy, but she remained a perfect corpse. My kiss hadn't been good enough; I hadn't been good enough. My hands balled into fists, my nails scraping the dirt. She'd only just claimed me as her own and now she had left me behind.

I lifted her head, squishing her cheeks between my palms. I screamed into her face, my tears falling across her nose, and then I dropped her head, a hollow thud against the earth.

Amelia's eyes blinked open. She rose onto her elbows and, in wonder, looked at the pond, the cabin, the soft sliver of moon already visible above the trees.

She looked at me.

"I'm here, mi amour," she said. "Don't be afraid."

✳

AT THE END OF the exit ramp, I turn right, although part of me thinks I should have gone left. I don't know the name of the street Orion is—*was*—on. No one ever thought it important to teach me.

I make a U-turn.

"Mom," Maya says. "You're driving like a maniac."

"Don't you have homework to do?"

She doesn't answer. I dangle my hand into the backseat. After a moment she takes hold of my fingers and squeezes.

"I used to live out here," I say, "when I was a kid."

"Where?"

"That's the problem. I can't remember."

"Grandma would know."

"We'll ask her, okay?" But I have no intention of asking Glory. Coming out here has been a mistake. If I found Orion, what would I do? Wander the path, calling Amelia's name?

"Don't tell Daddy about this," I say.

"Why not?"

"He'd think we were silly. I was silly."

"For not asking Grandma?"

"Right."

Maya lets go of my hand and curls up in the seat.

"Mi amour," I say.

"Okay, I won't tell Daddy."

When she brings her fingers to her mouth, I don't say a word.

four

PETER COMES HOME WHILE I'm making dinner. He is talking on the phone, always talking on the phone.

"We'll have to run the tests again," he says. "The data were all over the place."

I fill a pot with water, bang it on the stove.

"I wasn't there," he says, laughing.

I open a can of tomato sauce, the smell a poor imitation of the tomatoes Amelia and I picked—that smell of summer, the fruit supple in our hands, its flesh threatening to burst.

I stop myself. I can't keep doing this, moving back and forth in time.

"Carrie." Peter's hand cups the small of my back. "You okay?"

As I turn toward him, I consider telling him about the postcard, but he doesn't like what Amelia does to me, how she draws me away from him. From what he can understand.

"Yes," I say, smiling. "What's wrong with the tests?"

He groans. "Grad students. Well, one grad student. Completely incompetent."

"Pass him off."

"Her. I can't. She's doing my specialty."

The tests involve electrodes in mice. Peter swears the mice feel no pain. He and his students are learning about learning. In another study, he is learning about sleep. All this research, all this data, breaking down what we do every day unawares. It is beautiful, in a way, and horrible, too.

Tammy would have called what he does an atrocity.

But I don't. It's what I love about Peter—his curiosity, his scientific method, his calm assurances that of course the mice feel no pain, and most of all, my willingness to believe him.

Peter holds up two bags of pasta.

"Rigatoni," I say, and he dumps it into the water.

"I've been thinking," he says, giving the pot a pointless stir. "Maybe California is the right way to go."

I bite down on my lip as I shake oregano into the sauce. California is the last thing I want to talk about.

"You know how I feel about that," I say.

"Academia isn't the be all and—"

"You used to think so."

"When I was young and idealistic. Now I'm old and bitter, and with the budget cuts…You wouldn't believe the bullshit at the department meeting last week."

"But a drug company?"

"Wouldn't the extra money be nice?"

"I don't understand why it has to be California. If that's the way you have to do it, there are drug companies in Ohio, too."

"That's not where the offer is," Peter says, tightly.

"Maya would have to leave her friends."

"*I* changed schools."

"I did, too, and it was a nightmare."

The plates knock into each other as Peter takes them from the cupboard. "Your situation was different," he says.

"Don't do that. Don't pretend I don't have a frame of reference."

"Look." He holds out his hand. "Let's not do this tonight. Truce?"

As I put my hand in his, he pulls me into a kiss.

✳

After dinner Maya takes a bath and I stand in the hall and listen as she sings, her high voice echoing off the tiles and making my heart swell. She rarely sings anymore when she knows someone is listening.

Downstairs I hear Peter, on the phone again, and wish he were on the landline so I could pick up the extension, cover the mouthpiece with my hand.

"Want a story, mi amour?" I ask as I comb Maya's hair.

"I'll read my book," she says.

"Just one chapter, then lights out."

But I can't leave her. I lean against the headboard and look over her shoulder, following along to abridged *Anne of Green Gables*. On top of Maya's dresser, Samson, the mouse she "rescued" from Peter's lab, rustles the paper in his cage.

"Do you ever wish you had a brother or sister?" I say.

"Not really." Maya doesn't look up from her book.

"You don't get lonely?"

"I have friends."

"I know you do, but that's not the same as living with someone. Having someone always around."

She turns the page. "I like our family the way it is," she says.

"Good." I squeeze her shoulders.

five

I PUT THE POSTCARD with the others, hidden in the back pages of the Bible Peter's parents gave us as a wedding present. We'd laughed at their attempt to convert us, but secretly I thought the present sweet. After Maya was born, I wrote the date and time of her arrival inside the front cover, starting a historical record I hope will last for generations to come. That, I thought, had been the point of the present, not religious conversion: a tangible marker of our place in time, an object to be picked up and lifted into the future.

Eleven postcards—now twelve. I spread them out across the bed in chronological order, all but this last one with New York City postmarks, all but this last one images of the Brooklyn Bridge.

"She's keeping you under her control," Peter said after the fifth postcard, when we'd been married just over a year.

I agreed, but I wasn't sure I minded. When the next arrived in the mail a few months later, I didn't tell him. The postcards became my secret, and when they stopped, I had no one to confide in. I was about to give birth to Maya, and I convinced myself that I wanted Amelia to leave me alone, that somehow she understood my life and hers no longer had anything to do with each other. She was setting me free, and I was glad, finally, to be free.

But I kept the postcards. Alone in the house, I would take them out, line them up in order, count and recount. I'd check the backs for clues I had missed—an exaggerated slant to my name, a tremor in the zip code, a finesse to *Ohio*, never abbreviated, evidence of emotion, possible love. Proof of a meaningful connection that would elevate the mystery to more than just a cruel game, just a lonely woman in New York laughing at me lying on my bed, trying to decipher cheap postcards, stock images, her use of a different colored pen.

She could be watching the house right now. I get up, go to the window. The yards of my street, dark except for the glow of decorative streetlights, each one standing like a sentinel next to its driveway, muted yellow circles up and down the block.

I put my hand against the window. "Hello," I say, pressing my fingertips into the glass. "Hello."

✳

PETER UNDRESSES WITHOUT TURNING on the light. Ever fastidious, he folds his shirt and pants over his arm before putting them in the hamper. He is not a man to leave his underwear on the floor or whiskers in the sink, never even the seat up. Meanwhile, I am notorious for forgetting to close the kitchen cupboards. After dinner I looked over and saw three hanging, wide and unseemly.

Watching him tiptoe around the room, I consider opening the nightstand, taking out the Bible, shaking it over the bed and letting the postcards fly. I could take advantage of his guilt for being on the phone so late and turn it all into a joke. Look what I've been hiding from you; look how silly I've been.

"Awake," I say, and he gives a start.

I sit up but don't turn on the lamp.

"Was that a student?"

He climbs into bed without answering. I stare into the mirror above the dresser. Our shapes could be anyone. It's a comforting thought, that we could be any married couple, in any bedroom, in any house, anywhere in the world, our troubles not our own.

He lies on his side, facing me, and tugs on my arm, kisses my elbow, until I slide down beside him. There was a time I resented the students who would call, especially at night. I didn't understand why he needed to give out his cell phone number, why he couldn't leave the lectures for the classroom, the counseling for office hours, the mice for the lab. The female students have been the worst. Peter runs four days a week, keeps track of macronutrients, never touches alcohol or caffeine. He monitors his body with a biologist's cool fascination, and the result is a good-looking forty-four-year-old. I am not naive to the temptation, its flow in both directions, but those calls haven't come as often this year. Already his heart has moved on.

"Mark," he says, as I knew he would. Mark, the college buddy, now CEO of the drug company in Los Angeles, the name of which I refuse to commit to memory. I've met Mark twice, at our wedding and at their ten-year reunion. Both times he wore mirrored sunglasses indoors, drank too much wine, laughed too loudly. He had a different woman with him each time, although I mistook them for the same person. Petite redheads wearing too much makeup, stuffed into too tight dresses, teetering on too high heels, clutching his arm so they wouldn't fall over. As the evenings wore on, I heard him call them by different names and wondered if they were escorts. When I asked Peter, he got angry. Sophomore to senior year, Mark had been his roommate and best friend.

"Have you picked out the house yet?" I say.

"Carrie." He starts in again on my elbow. I've seen him looking; he hasn't even tried to hide it. The three of us on the sofa, watching TV, and Peter has his laptop open, combing through real estate sites. Spanish style. Bungalow. Pools hypnotically blue. New construction, glass houses—those who live in glass houses...

What bothers me most is his confidence: he has imagined a California life for us, already moved us there in his mind. I've checked the pages he's bookmarked. His preferences run new and expensive. Sterile. I could never soften those interiors, no matter how many rugs and pillows and drapes I piled on. That's not the point of a house like that. Those aren't homes. They're stages on which to perform.

A glass house can shatter. The log cabins Robert and Mike built withstood tornado winds, golf-ball sized hail. They could still be standing, even now, those structures built by four hands.

My face tightens, the gathering of tears. I turn my head away and let them snake down my nose and disappear into the pillow.

"Just keep an open mind," Peter says. "That's all I ask."

Soon he will have to notify the department that he won't be coming back in the fall. A decision will have to be made, and I will be a good wife, or a bad wife.

He puts his arm around my waist. His hand falls over my mine, and I feel the outline of his ring. We got married at the Cleveland Botanical Garden, bees buzzing around our heads. Glory walked me down the aisle. Coupling and uncoupling. Glory lifting my hand, passing it to Peter, closing his fingers around my fingers.

Here she is. Just for you. Take her.

"Who was your first love?" I ask.

He laughs under his breath, ready for sleep. "Jackie Johnson," he says. "Seventh grade."

I've heard the story of Jackie Johnson before. The first girl he asked on a date. She had dark hair, wore an orange sundress. They went to the movies, and her dad sat in the row behind them. Jackie Johnson isn't the kind of love I meant.

I wait for Peter to ask me, but he doesn't. I feel the absence of the question, a hollow in my stomach. My muscles tighten, and his arm responds, drawing back so his hand rests on my hip. He is afraid of my answer. He carries the shame of my past as if it were a stain, marking him, in danger of smearing up the walls of our glass house.

six

I watched her, the product of Tammy's vision, something I could never be: a child raised completely removed from the corruptions and temptations of SAS. Although my family had been vegan for as long as I could remember, my life before Orion had contained most of the creature comforts: a two-story house with a pink bedroom for me, a closet full of clothes bought at the mall, cartoons on Saturday mornings and sitcoms after dinner, a whole group of friends from Montessori preschool who came over for play dates and invited me to birthday parties at skating rinks and pizza parlors (I'd bring along a vegan meal in my Barbie lunch box, but several other kids brought their own peanut-free or sugar-free foods, too). Sometimes Mike would sneak me a hot dog or a can of Cherry Coke when we ran Sunday errands. Once he bought us cream-filled doughnuts iced with chocolate, which we ate sitting on the hood of the car in the K-Mart parking lot. I remember being mesmerized; he chewed with his eyes closed. An hour later my stomach cramped, but I thought about those doughnuts for a long time. I made him promise to buy me one again, but he never did.

Tammy hoped Amelia would rub off on me. Amelia was not afraid of going to the outhouse in the middle of the night; she didn't have nightmares about falling into the composting toilet. She could meditate for hours at a time; only I knew she'd trained herself to sleep sitting up. She never complained about hauling water from Home or weeding the vegetable garden on blazing hot afternoons. No one seemed to notice the biscuits she stole or, when we were a little older, the sips she took from the jug of homebrew that Calvin in Cabin C kept hidden from Tammy beneath his porch.

I took a sip, but only after she'd told me the brew tasted like my favorite thing, strawberries warmed in the sun. She laughed as I spat into the grass. When I looked up, I saw Calvin standing in the doorway. He and Amelia grinned at each other.

"That wasn't funny," I said.

Calvin cackled like a crow and stepped back into his cabin.

"You've got to pretend," Amelia said, almost apologetically.

✳

THOSE FIRST FEW WEEKS at Orion, I often found Glory and Mike's bedroom door closed in the middle of the afternoon. I would squat on the floor and listen to the sounds they made: Glory's guttural purr, Mike's spastic grunt. Crouching there, I felt like a spy, gathering important information that would solve a mystery. But the noises, when they were loud, embarrassed me and made me uneasy. I'd dig my fingers into the spaces between the floorboards and imagine bursting in, the way Glory had done when my cousin spent the night at our old house and we stayed up giggling past bedtime. Just like her, I'd place my hands on my hips and shout, "Cut it out, you two!"

But I knew if I opened the door, what I would see would be even more disturbing than the sounds. As Glory's whimpers faded, their talking began, their voices low and caressing, solicitous. They were bad approximations of the voices I knew, as if aliens had beamed down, taken over my parents' bodies, and were trying out human speech for the first time.

One day the door opened. I slid back into the corner as Glory came out, naked. As she padded over to the water bucket, I stared at her wiggling backside, the furrows of cellulite along her upper thighs, the indentation like two thumb prints at the small of her back. Her stomach protruded past her hip bones in a low, soft bulge, and her breasts hung like deflated balloons, her nipples erect, her areoles dark. She filled a mug with water and drank, water dripping down her chin. When she looked up, she saw me looking at her.

"Baby," Mike called in his alien voice from the bedroom.

Glory set her mug down on top of the woodstove. "What are you doing here?" she said.

"What's that?" Mike said. "Who's here?"

I pressed my back against the wall joint. The sun flooded through the window above, spreading warmth across my knees. Glory's pubic hair, darker than the hair on her head, was thick and curly. She had thick hair underneath her arms, too.

"Shouldn't you be out playing with Amelia?" she said.

A thump came from the bedroom. Mike appeared in the doorway in his boxer shorts. "Shit," he said. "How long have you been out here?"

I noted his pale, flabby stomach. Robert's stomach was hard and brown. He dove into the pond after Amelia and me, splashing us, lifting us into the air as if we weighed nothing at all. Sometimes I fantasized about drowning in the pond and Robert jumping in to save me.

Mike looked at Glory. "Put some clothes on," he said.

"She's already seen me. Besides, she's going to be a woman someday." Turning toward me, Glory straightened her shoulders and squared her hips. "She ought to see what a woman's body looks like."

I stared at my mother. Standing that way, she looked like Wonder Woman, ready to save the day.

"How long have you been here?" Mike asked again.

"I don't know," I said.

"Right." He ran a hand through his hair. "Do you have questions? About what you heard?"

I shook my head and stuffed my fingertips deep between the floorboards. The wood pinched. If I pulled my fingers out too quickly, I'd get a splinter and Mike would pick me up and carry me to the first aid kit where we kept the tweezers. He would sing a nonsense song as he yanked the splinter out fast. I squinted, preparing to cry, and pulled my fingers out of the floor. They came away unscathed.

"Maybe you should show her your body, too," Glory said.

Mike pulled the waistband of his boxers higher. "You've got to be kidding."

"No, think about it. We're her teachers now. If she doesn't learn from us, she never will. The human body is beautiful." Glory leaned toward me, her breasts dangling. "The human body is nothing to be ashamed of, Carrie."

I covered my face with my hands.

"You're embarrassing her," Mike said.

"We should ask Tammy about this."

"What? Now?"

"We're obviously doing this wrong." She grabbed my wrists. "Carrie, please look at me."

But I didn't want to look. I twisted out of her grasp and stumbled out of the cabin, down the porch steps. Only when I reached the safety of earth did I uncover my eyes.

Amelia's red shirt gave her away. Her feet trailed the water as her hands braided blades of pond grass into a circle. "I'm weaving a basket," she said as I plunked down beside her.

"Can I help?"

"Sure. I want some of the yellow grass. Over there."

I crawled to the spot she had indicated. "These ones?"

"Yeah. Pick two. Make sure they're strong."

When I brought the blades back, she smiled and thanked me. I watched as she expertly wove them in.

"Glory and Mike," I said.

She looked up, her hands still moving.

"I heard them," I said.

"Heard them what?"

But I didn't know how to tell her. Out here, beneath the bright sun, what had gone on inside the dim cabin seemed distant, muddled. I wasn't sure it had really happened at all.

"You know," I said. "Doing it."

"You mean making love?" She laughed. "Making love isn't bad. It's natural for adults to do. Tammy says it's healthy, like exercise. If they go too long without it, they get mean."

As usual she had all the answers. I'd come to her knowing she would, yet her confidence annoyed me, made me feel like a baby.

"But I don't want to hear them," I said. "I don't want to see."

"Then don't hang around when they're making love. You have free will, Carrie."

One of Tammy's favorite phrases.

"Don't let your negative energy bring down their positive."

That was another.

The grass moved over and under Amelia's fingers. When the basket was done, she would give it to Tammy, who would sell it, along with the mugs and vases she made on the wheel outside of Cabin A and the wooden whistles Robert carved, to a store in Peninsula.

"Can we stop talking about it?" I said.

"See that dragonfly over there?" Amelia pointed with her elbow. "Do you know why it has that name?"

I shook my head.

"Because it's descended from dragons. If you got really close, you'd see that its body is just like a dragon's body, with a pointed nose and scales and everything. When we aren't looking, dragonflies breathe fire."

"Why not when we're looking?"

"Silly. They don't want us to know."

"I'd like to see."

"Maybe we'll sneak up on one. But you'll have to be really quiet. You'll have to do exactly as I say or else you'll scare it away just like you're always doing with the deer."

"I'm getting better with that," I said.

"Yes," she said. "You are."

She began to hum, high and tuneless, a trait she'd inherited from Robert, their happiness bubbling over with no effort, no self-consciousness. My shoulders relaxed, my thighs eased into the mud. I dipped my toes into the pond, something I would never do if I were out here alone. Whenever I walked by myself, I gave the pond's clouded waters a wide berth.

✳

"You girls," Tammy said, "are very lucky."

In the meeting room Amelia and I sat side-by-side on child-size chairs, hers yellow, mine red. Tammy sat on top of the bookshelf, which Robert had built and painted new-leaf green. On the shelves were our books, the ones purchased from the thrift store and the ones Tammy had written herself and illustrated on thick sheets of recycled paper. Those were my favorites. The book about spring with the budding flowers and baby animals; the book about fall with the plants going to sleep, not dying. One book was about the phases of the moon and another about our bodies and how the Earth gave us good food to grow strong. Everything was connected, Tammy had taught us. Each person, each animal, each twig, each petal, each drop of rain, each stone. We were all one, all sacred, and so we had to be kind to each other.

Tammy loved us, her second chances.

"Out there," she said, "children's minds are being poisoned. They're shrinking, shriveling up to nothing, before they ever have the chance to grow."

She swung her bare feet. Her patchwork skirt reminded me of a rainbow, of the flowers that grew from Sara's ashes.

"Those SAS children forget the precious secrets the universe whispered in their ears. They see too much, hear too much, and all of it lies. Blasphemy. They are robbed of themselves before they're out of the womb."

She hopped down from the bookshelf and knelt before of us, her rough hands cradling the backs of our heads.

"But not you two. You two will always be pure. Promise me that."

"We promise," Amelia said and looked at me.

"We promise," I said.

"Dear ones, will you stay close?"

Amelia touched the perfume ball Tammy wore on a green ribbon around her neck, rolling the pendant back and forth across Tammy's bony chest.

"Always," Amelia said.

"You, dearest, have been given special gifts. I am counting on you to do great things."

Amelia's poems decorated the meeting room walls. Meanwhile, I still struggled to compose complete sentences.

"You have been blessed with an active imagination," Tammy said. "A way with words. Charisma. You must take these talents and use them to tell the truth. You must make people listen."

"What about me?" I said.

"Yes," Tammy said, "what about you? What do you want from this life?"

What I wanted was to stay right here in the meeting room forever, learning about the world and our special place inside it, enveloped by the gentle warmth of my teacher and my best friend.

"I'll tell the truth, too," I said.

"Our little parrot." Tammy cupped my chin in her hand. "Someday won't you want to fly on your own?"

"Why?" I said.

She laughed. "Why?" She gave my chin a shake. "Why, indeed. Well, little parrot, parrot away."

seven

WHAT MOST ATTRACTED ME to Peter was his certainty. He could walk into a room and with a single, scanning look size up the people, evaluate the situation, and form a neat, accurate conclusion. As a twenty-two year old secretary in the biology department, I found this confident Ph.D. student with the carriage of a professor impressive. My being there was a fluke. When I'd graduated from college the year before, I'd taken the first job that came my way, administrative work in the Registrar's office. Then one of the biology secretaries needed eye surgery, and I went where I was sent.

"Fate," I liked to tease him.

"Fate," he said, "is our way of discounting the randomness of the universe."

Or, "If you hadn't found your fate with me, you would have found it with someone else."

"Still," I said, "what a nice coincidence."

I had a small apartment above an old carriage house that was a short bus ride or long walk from campus. That fall I liked to walk. Watching Cleveland turn to gold around me, I felt uplifted, an adult now, in control of my destiny.

Peter was nothing like the boys I'd dated in college, those musicians and painters and skateboarders who wore anti-establishment t-shirts, tried to grow magic mushrooms in their closets, and sold pot to pay the rent. As Peter leaned over my desk and asked if I would like to go to dinner, I had a sudden flash of Robert leaning over the meeting room table, giving me encouragement as I worked an algebra problem. Physically, Peter did not resemble Robert. He was pale and slight where Robert was dark and broad. Yet the straightness of his shoulders, the relaxed hang of his arms, projected the sturdy steadiness I'd come to rely on in my childhood.

Peter smelled good, too. Like old leather-bound books and shaving cream.

We went to a bar close to campus. Over hamburgers I asked about his studies. He explained that he was a behavioral biologist and opened his messenger bag, took out a folder containing columns of numbers, graphs, tallies, the statistical analysis of three semesters' work.

"My dissertation is on stress tolerance," he said. "Which secondary conditions exacerbate the fight-or-flight response and which lessen it."

I followed the curve of a line with my finger. I liked the idea of stress being reduced to a number, to points on a graph. I wondered what else he could reduce this way: anger, sadness, fear? What about love? The possibilities seemed endless.

"What do you want to do with this?" I said.

He hesitated, his shyness unexpected, a flattering surprise. I noticed he had barely touched his drink. Mine was almost gone.

"Ultimately," he said, "I'm interested in practical uses. I'd like to be of help. I'm thinking about people in high-stress professions. Firemen, cops, soldiers. Social workers. Or victims of domestic violence. Children. The terminally ill and their families. How can we lessen these responses in them?"

It was a good answer. Sitting across from me, I saw a good man.

I placed my hands over his. Above our table, a lamp made from an old oil tin spotlighted our intertwined fingers. We didn't speak for several minutes. The bar was crowded, noisy, students and faculty members settling into their Friday night. In the corner a flashing jukebox played Aerosmith.

✳

I WAITED UNTIL OUR fourth date to tell him about Amelia.

We'd come to my apartment after dinner and were sitting on the sofa, drinking cups of chamomile tea. ("No coffee," Peter said. "I like to keep my mind clean.") The heat had yet to come on, and we shared an afghan, a large sunflower spread over our laps. I picked at the cotton, the taste of garlic from the pasta sauce lingering on my tongue.

Why did I choose that moment? My best excuse is that I had a flash of foresight. With my thigh pressed against his, I felt like an old married couple, cozy and comfortable together. This could be our life, and if this were our life, he would need to know who I was.

I told him about Orion. I told him about my best friend.

"We were like sisters," I said. "But more than that. We were two parts of the same person."

"Which part were you?" he said.

"The bad part."

"So Amelia was the good?"

"Not exactly." Sara was the good. I wanted to tell him about her, but I didn't know how to fit her in, how to make her make sense. "Amelia wasn't perfect, but she was better than me. She was beautiful and confident and smart. She was so creative."

His fingers paraded up and down my thigh. "*You're* beautiful," he said.

I gave him a look.

"Where is she now?" he asked.

"I don't know," I said and without warning started to cry.

He put his mug on the floor and held me.

"I feel stupid," I said.

"No." His lips brushed the top of my head. "You're anything but that."

I thought about the numbers lined up in rows, the percentages and bell curves. I wanted my life to be lined up, too, neat and orderly and understandable.

I twisted around and kissed him. His lips were so eager that briefly I was taken aback before I remembered that I had initiated and undid his belt buckle. We made fast, deliberate love and fell asleep right there on the sofa. Toward morning the heat banged through the pipes, rudely waking us. We moved to the bed—Peter frowned as he pushed aside my dirty, tangled sheets; soon he would take to washing them and making the bed himself—but I could not fall back to sleep. I got up and, naked, cooked pancakes from a mix. The batter splattered my stomach, but the sensation wasn't entirely unpleasant. I felt useful, competent—like a fully-grown woman—in my kitchen. While I cooked Peter took a book from his bag and read propped up on the sofa, his nose close to the page, highlighting often.

As an early snow fell, transforming the street into a blank, I watched him and thought: The only two in the world.

eight

You fall the hardest for your first love. It's unfair to compare those who come after. Unfair but unavoidable.

While we were dating, Peter bought me a book about children raised in isolation. Feral children with delayed development and no social skills. A wolf girl. A boy kept locked in a cupboard. The book fascinated and repulsed me; their stories made me angry.

"Not one," I said. "Two."

"Thank God for that."

I threw the book away.

That night I pretended to be feral. I pounced on the bed, sniffed his hair, pawed at his chest. I snarled. Bit him on the neck. When he reached for me, I ran off into the corner and curled up in the darkness, whimpering. He dragged me back to bed and held me down. I fought until the bitter end. In the morning we inspected our wounds. I kissed the places where I had drawn blood, and we made love sweetly, the wolf girl tamed.

Later we would laugh about that night, embarrassed and ashamed but also intrigued by the possibilities. One of us would growl, and it would send us both into hysterics. But that was all we could do, make that night into a joke. We never dared venture there again.

nine

IN MY MIND AMELIA exists in a black-and-white movie, the New York City Poet, Audrey Hepburn's spunky elegance with Sylvia Plath's haunting malaise. I see her carrying a paper grocery bag, a loaf of French bread and bouquet of wildflowers peeking out the top, as she walks down tree-lined streets to her brownstone apartment, her pretty features tight with thought. She sits at sidewalk cafés and writes in a Moleskine notebook, pausing occasionally to press her pen to her lips and gaze out at the city, seeing without seeing. In cavernous Greenwich Village bars, she stands on a stage and recites, everyone leaning forward, captivated by her words.

Always she is alone. I try to give her a man, a young Bob Dylan lookalike. I have them reenact the famous cover pose, her as Suze Rotolo, gripping his arm and grinning, her excitement barely contained as they set off together on a New York life. I feel generous holding this image, but it's false. Solitude had been the point. "New York," she told me the last time I saw her, "where I can be no one."

✳

AT WORK I LET the cursor blink inside the Google rectangle. Again and again, I type and delete the letters of her name. I'm not sure which would be worse: news of her suffering or a Facebook page with a thousand friends. Either way, I wouldn't know what to do. I can't send her an email and invite her into my life; I can't send her an email and risk her not answering.

I google myself instead, to see what she has seen. There isn't much. My profile on LinkedIn. I scroll through my employment history, rising through the ranks from administrative assistant to office manager. An uninspired list. A lack of ambition, she would think, and she might be right, but I haven't cared. Until now.

My address is easy to find, my phone number, too. There's my name alongside Peter, Maya, even Glory. I click on a link and see our home at street level. I zoom out, and there we are, the little red marker just over halfway between New York and Chicago.

✳

Sara.
355 Harper Avenue.
Apartment 2B.
Chicago.

A dozen times a day, the address runs through my head. My lips move, my private prayer.

Sara.
355 Harper Avenue.
Apartment 2B.
Chicago.

✳

SOME DAYS I'M NOT generous. Some days I'm angry.

How dare you, I think as I throw the mail—no postcard

again—toward the counter and fall short, envelopes and catalogues scattering across the floor.

How dare you, I think as I drink smoothies with Maya at the mall and grow indignant at the story she's telling, a slight at the end-of-year party by a classmate, bossy and arrogant like Amelia, and Maya's eyes widen, my reaction too fierce. "Mom," she says, "it's fine. We're over it."

"Friends like that aren't real friends," I say.

"We all have bad days," she says, something I have told her before. Be generous, I've taught her. Be kind. Try to see the other perspective.

"You don't have to put up with it. You can walk away."

"I *did* walk away," Maya says.

"I don't just mean in the moment. You can walk away forever. Sometimes that's the best thing to do."

She raises her eyebrows, her straw squeaking against her cup as she sucks up the last of the smoothie.

"You forgot the lemon bars," she says.

"Shit," I say before I catch myself. "I'm sorry, mi amour."

"It's all right. I just figured you had a bad day."

My daughter—she's a smart one.

"Bad spring, more like," I say.

She pats my hand.

"I really don't mind," she says. "I think they're kind of gross anyway."

✳

MAYA'S FRIEND SOPHIE COMES over, and they take the sidewalk chalk outside to draw on the driveway. I watch from the front steps, the book I've been reading all spring open to a random page on my lap. Every time I see a figure moving toward us, I look up, my heart stopping before I realize that it's just Phyllis O'Leary walking her greyhound, Annie Schott jogging, the teenage Hernandez boy on his bike. A sudden breeze rustles the leaves, messes up the girls' hair. They shriek and come toward me with hands spread wide, a second skin yellow, green, blue.

Summer

one

FATHER'S DAY SNEAKS UP on me. I am never good at remembering, despite the window displays, the advertisements on the radio.

"Look what I made," Maya says when I pick her up at Glory's.

"Soap?" I say, and Glory shrugs.

"It was a kit," she says.

The bars are lumpy, mottled gray, and smell like laundry detergent.

"Daddy will love these," I say, knowing he will tell her that and never use them. Peter has his body wash, his face cream, specially selected for their pH balance. Maya's soap bars will collect dust in the cabinet below the sink until eventually I throw them out.

The next day, after work, I wander through the bookstore, past tables piled high with books on golfing and football, with saccharine little volumes on being daddy's little girl or having the world's best dad.

"May I help you?"

At the end of the table he materializes, the resemblance so shocking that for several seconds, I lose the ability to speak.

"I've seen you circle this table three times," he says. "Is there something in particular you're looking for?"

His hands are Robert's hands, but smoother. Robert's hands in a gentler life. The long fingers run down a stack of fishing guides, aligning the spines.

"A gift," I say.

"For your father?"

"My husband."

He places one hand on top of the fishing guides, the other on his hip. I read his nametag. "Jeff," I say. "You have to help me."

"What's your husband interested in?"

I laugh. "California."

"We have travel guides."

"No. God, no. Anything but that."

Jeff looks at me quizzically.

"I'd like to see your poetry section," I say.

As I follow him down the aisles, I feel as if I'm floating. My skin tingles, the pins and needles of half-sleep, the way I used to feel coming out of long meditation, my body becoming sensitized to the world again, my eyes suddenly seeing things as they really are.

"Amelia Holbrook," I say.

He squats to look at the lower shelves. "Holbrook, Holbrook. Yep. Here you go."

The book, a sign, at least, if not a miracle. When I don't move to take it, he lifts it higher, and I grab hold. On the cover an apple head doll, like the ones Tammy made for us, slumps against a black background. *Forced Silences.* The title seems a rebuke, but it can't be, not toward me personally. How would she ever know I would see it?

I check the copyright. The book is two years old.

"I've never read her stuff," Jeff says. "Our new manager is a poetry freak. I'm trying to expand my knowledge. I like John Berryman."

"He's good," I say. The book is dedicated to *SH.* Sara.

On the back is the same author photograph as on her first collection. Amelia forever twenty-seven. When her first book came out, Glory called me with the title and publisher, and I drove to three different bookstores before I found the slim volume with the plain red cover. I went to the coffeehouse next door, ordered a chai latte, and tucked into the velour window seat, feeling both excitement and dread, turned to the first page. Amelia's words of truth. Her images were simple and stark, set off by blank spaces, winding from line to broken-off line, stanza to unfinished stanza, poems ending where they should have begun, beginning where they should have ended.

Page after page leading me in circles.

"Is there anything else I can do for you?"

"No," I say. "This is great."

When I look up, Jeff is grinning at me. He looks less like Robert than I originally thought. More like Amelia.

"I'm Carrie," I say and hold out my hand. "I really can't thank you enough."

On the way home I stop at the 7-Eleven and buy a box of chocolates. For Mother's Day, Peter gave me waxy tulips. I call it even.

✳

an overturned teacup with

out a handle

forced silences

the fullness of our histories

drunk

both of us have been left

alone too

long

"What are you reading?" Maya says.

I lift up the edge of the afghan, and she crawls in next to me, rests her head on my shoulder. Her hair is wet, the comb strokes visible; she smells of vanilla soap and pomegranate shampoo. Peter is working late at the lab again, and so we had a pizza dinner, the third this week. The box still sits on the coffee table, although I did clear away the paper plates, their bottoms soggy with grease, and made sure Maya ate a few baby carrots, too.

"My friend wrote this," I say.

Maya bends the book toward her. "Which friend?"

"From a long time ago. When I was your age."

" 'An overturned teacup with,' " Maya reads. She tilts her head, as if contemplating a painting. "That doesn't make sense."

"Keep going."

" 'Out a handle. Forced silences.' " She shudders. "I don't think I like this."

I close the book. I don't like it either—Maya's child-voice reading Amelia's words of loneliness.

"What's her name?" Maya takes the book from me. "Amelia Holbrook." She smiles. "Amelia. I like that name. Like Amelia Bedelia. Or that woman in the plane they never found."

"Earhart. Shouldn't you be getting ready for bed?"

"Not yet." She turns to Amelia's picture on the back cover. "She's pretty. Why haven't I met her?"

"She lives in New York," I say, but I sound like I'm making excuses. "We haven't really been friends for many, many years."

Maya flips through the pages. I grab the book with more force than I intended. My job: to keep all forms of sadness away.

"Bed," I say. "Now."

I fold the afghan into a neat rectangle and let her gape, but my authority has its limits and she knows what they are. I go into the kitchen and get us each a cookie. She nibbles around the edges, a habit she has had since toddlerhood, and goes upstairs without complaint.

I don't remind her to brush her teeth even though I see specks of chocolate as I bend down to kiss her good night.

She tucks the blanket around her shoulders, forming a little burrow the way I have always liked to sleep.

"You," I say, "are my world."

✳

WITH MY CHILD TUCKED in and my husband working late with his cyborg mice and incompetent grad students, I close my bedroom door and prop Amelia's last postcard up against the alarm clock. I bring the scrap of notebook paper to my nose and inhale, searching for traces of Amelia, Robert, Tammy. I want to smell the woods, the pond, the dirt, even the warm compost outside the Home kitchen door. But the paper smells of nothing.

I think about Jeff's hands, neatening the stacks of books, pulling Amelia's from the shelf. His strong grip as his hand took mine.

Those square palms. Those long fingers.

Robert's hands were calloused, stained by the tools of his trades: dirt, motor oil, pinesap, berries. When he spoke, he moved his hands together and apart, swooping to the side, projecting upward, with elegance and precision. If I closed my eyes and just listened to his voice—low toned, soft even when he was yelling—I felt as if I were missing whole sentences, entire paragraphs. I felt guilty. He was our greatest teacher, and I wanted to absorb everything he had to teach me.

I feel as if a pressure valve has been released. As if I've come Home. My breath finds its natural rhythm for the first time in weeks, and I spread out on the bed, stretch my arms and legs, rotate my wrists and ankles, enjoying the simple pleasure of breathing.

two

THAT FIRST DAY, ROBERT squatted in front of me so he could look me in the eye. "We'll take good care of you," he said.

He wore baggy jeans and a plaid shirt, the sleeves rolled up, the muscles on his forearms as distinct and smooth as stones. He looked nothing like my grandfathers, who were bald and fat and wore golf shirts and loafers. His blue eyes drilled into mine until I had to look away.

Amelia leaned her elbow on Robert's back, her chin propped on her hand, his arm slung low around her waist. Mike sometimes held my hand, but I had to offer it first. He was never the type of father to lift me into his lap or swing me up onto his shoulders.

"You and my dad built the cabin," I said.

"That's right."

"I didn't know he could do that."

Robert laughed—a deep, throaty sound. I hadn't intended to be funny, but felt a swelling pride that I had been, that I'd pleased him.

"Neither did I," he said. "And neither did he. Do you like it?"

I nodded, even though I hadn't set foot inside yet. The sudden fear that the interior of my family's cabin looked nothing like Amelia's gripped me. What if there were holes in the floor? What if the roof sagged? What if Mike's efforts had been an embarrassment, Robert dragging him along, doing what he could to fix the mistakes?

But Robert's face conveyed only kindness. When he smiled, deep lines formed around the sides of his mouth.

"Good," he said. "We built it just for you."

"And for Glory," Amelia said.

"And for Glory, too."

"And for all of us."

"Yes, for all of us, because you coming here has made all our lives better. Especially mi amour's."

I wanted to believe him.

That evening I sat between Amelia and Robert on their porch as we sucked on popsicles, blueberries frozen in water. The sun set over the trees, and the fireflies came out, flashing over the pond and among the grasses. Back at my old house, I would catch fireflies and put them in a jelly jar, falling asleep with them flickering beside my bed and waking to their shriveled bodies. I'd flush them down the toilet, but a few days later, I would forget and capture more. Here, I could already guess that catching fireflies would be wrong. I didn't even make the suggestion, and in my reticence, I felt growth. I was changing into someone new, someone content to sit with Robert and Amelia, our lips sticky, and count the flashes.

Amelia asked Robert to tell us the story of Sara's ashes, the field of flowers.

"So you've met her?" he said to me.

By then Sara had become as real to me as either one of them.

He leaned back on his elbows. "Violets," he said. "Larkspur. Coneflowers. Hollyhocks."

Each word lingered, distilled by the twilight.

"Foxglove," Amelia said. "Dahlias."

"Snapdragons. Jack-in-the-Pulpit."

I knew violets, but none of the others. The names sounded magical, a spell being cast. I leaned back, eased by Robert's steady incantation. Amelia rested her head against my shoulder, her scalp smelling of the heat of the day. Her eyelashes fluttered against my arm.

"She had a good heart," Robert said. "When you have a good heart, you can make anything happen."

"*I* have a good heart," Amelia said.

Robert wrapped his hand around the back of her neck, his

fingers brushing against the base of my spine. "It's getting better," he said.

Glory came slowly around the pond, her fingers trailing through the grasses, her eyes focused on the fall of her feet. I hadn't seen her since Amelia led me away that morning. Back at home I would follow her through the house, consumed by anxiety bubbling in the pit of my stomach, boiling over whenever she and Mike fought. She would yell at me to please, please give her space and lock herself in the bathroom with a magazine. I'd wait outside the door, listening to her turn the pages. Today, for hours, I'd forgotten her existence.

"All moved in?" Robert said.

Glory stopped, startled.

"It's beautiful here," she said.

"Nowhere else like it."

Glory leaned against the railing, her arms crossed low over her stomach. Her hair curled around her face the way it did when she'd been sweating. "Hi there, sweetheart," she said. "We haven't seen you all day."

She placed her hand on my knee, her fingers rigid, claws. I scooted closer to Amelia. Glory tucked my hair behind my ears.

"I already feel at home," she said. "We couldn't have made a better choice for our family."

"You won't regret coming here," Robert said.

"Regret?" Glory took a step back. "I don't even like to think about that word. No more." She crossed her arms in front of her, swept them apart. "Life's too short, right? We might all die tomorrow."

"Something like that," Robert said.

The next day, when Glory found out about Sara's death, she regretted her choice of words. She avoided Robert until she had to face him across the dining table at Home. Over steaming plates of roasted potatoes and mashed lentils, she could not stop apologizing.

"I have no idea what you're talking about," Robert said, forking kale on to his plate. "You have been nothing but friendliness and grace."

Seated beside Glory, I gripped the edge of my chair, willing her to be quiet. The rest of the commune—a dozen members then—went on eating, but I could sense them leaning forward, listening with perked up ears.

"Your daughter," Glory said. "I didn't know. She was so young. I can't imagine what you—"

"It's the worst thing in the world to lose a child," Tammy said from the head of the table. Her gray hair hung in two thick braids, her face wrinkled and severe. Barely five feet tall, the bones of her shoulders and elbows and wrists poking through her leathery skin, Tammy dominated the room. Even Robert seemed to shrink by comparison.

Glory pinched the skin at the base of her throat. "If I lost Carrie," she said, "I'd die myself."

"That's an exaggeration," Tammy said. "You don't die. Dying is cowardly. You have to accept that you are alive and persevere."

"Enough talk of death," Robert said.

Beneath the table, Amelia kicked my shins, but I ignored her. I sensed the tension in Glory's body; she wasn't finished yet.

"Please," she said. "Just accept my apology."

"Accepted and ejected," Robert said around a mouthful of potatoes.

When I lifted my head, he winked at me.

three

I TELL PETER THAT I'm taking an early evening yoga class and meet Jeff at his apartment, a dingy studio above a bicycle repair shop a few towns over. The sex is quick, furtive, necessary. I imagine us as two squirrels, hidden in the high up branches of a tree, mating because our bodies are in heat, the season changing soon.

It's nothing like I thought it would be, and it's better that way.

Afterward he wants me to shower with him, but I say I have to pick up my daughter. I dress while he lies in bed, his hand reaching for me whenever I pass by.

"Thank you," I say. When I bend down to kiss him, he turns his head away. Clearly, I am the bad guy.

I intend to shower when I get home, but I am running late, Glory's car already in the driveway, Peter due back soon. As I make dinner, the smell of illicit sex on my skin, I feel more energized than guilty.

In bed I fling myself on Peter, wedge my tongue into his mouth, pin down his shoulders, grind my hips against his. I am the wolf girl, but this time he doesn't try to tame me.

Afterward he laughs up at the ceiling. "What," he says, "has gotten into you?"

"Summer," I say.

four

AT THE BEGINNING OF our eight-year-old October, Robert taught us how to shoot. He had a bow and a decaying quiver of arrows from when he was a boy; we would aim only at the trees, and we wouldn't tell Tammy.

"Do you think this is a good idea?" Glory asked the morning we were to begin lessons. I sat between her and Mike on the cabin floor, a bowl of oatmeal between my legs. Mike hadn't finished building our table yet. Out back leaned an old door recovered from a demolished church, waiting since spring to be sanded.

"Archery is sport," Mike said. "They'll strengthen their hand-eye coordination."

"Still." Glory moved her hand away from her spoon, which stayed sticking straight up in the center of her bowl. Tammy knew how to thin oatmeal with freshly made soymilk, adding a dash of cinnamon or a handful of chopped apple, but lately Glory had stopped letting us eat breakfast at Home. She woke early and cooked oatmeal on the woodstove, moving with angular, darting gestures, stoking the fire too much, sending clouds of smoke into the room. When she finished, her shirt was askew, her eyes bright.

"Don't worry," Mike said. "We won't get into trouble. Robert's been here since the dawn of time."

"Carrie." Glory lowered onto one elbow and looked me straight in the eye. "Do you want to learn to shoot?"

I put the empty spoon in my mouth, fitting the curve around my tongue, and shrugged. I just wanted to be with Amelia and Robert.

"It's harmless fun," Mike said.

Glory leaned against the wall. "I don't want to get this wrong," she said.

Placing his palms on the floor, Mike heaved himself up. He rose more awkwardly than Robert, though Robert was fifteen years older. I had taken to making a running list of all the ways Mike and Glory did not measure up. The tally soothed me, even if none of their shortcomings seemed likely to be compensated.

As Mike started for the door, Glory grabbed his shin.

"Jesus," he said, pitching forward, his bowl landing upside down on the floor next to me, splattering the wall with oatmeal. "What is wrong with you?"

"Fine," Glory said, letting go of his leg. "I guess she might as well learn from the best."

A few weeks earlier Glory had told me that Robert had been a sniper in Vietnam. She'd used the hushed, slightly embarrassed, slightly joyful tone she took when gossiping—as if she knew what she was doing was wrong but could not resist.

I hadn't understood what she meant.

"He killed people," she'd said

"That's not true."

"You don't know, Carrie. People are different here than they were before."

She started to say something else, but Tammy came around the corner carrying a garbage bag full of old clothes for us to tear into strips. The strips would be traded to Lori McConnell, who'd use them to make rugs, and in exchange we'd get food from their farm.

Now Glory pulled me into her lap and began braiding my hair. Her fingers moved quickly, roughly. She stopped and undid her work, beginning again more gently, smoothing the hair at the crown of my head, letting her fingers pause after each twist, as if reminding herself that she did this because she cared for me. I stared at the strip of light underneath the cabin door and waited for Robert and Amelia to come to my rescue.

Glory was halfway done with the second braid when the door

swung open and Robert leaned into the room. Behind him on the porch, Calvin sang a song about railroads with Amelia balanced on his hip.

"Morning," Robert said. "I'd come in, but I've got my boots on."

I scampered out of Glory's lap.

"Wait," she said. "We're not done."

Bending at the waist, I shook my head until the braids flew apart.

"They were sloppy anyway," Glory said and began stacking bowls.

"Morning Glory!" Calvin shouted.

She looked at Robert. "Be safe."

"You have my word," Robert said.

"You know I'll hold you to it."

"I wouldn't expect anything else, Mama Bear."

"Take your coat," Glory said.

I lifted my jacket from the hook beside the door and raced outside, where Amelia jumped up and down the porch steps. Calvin had already started for the woods, the quiver of arrows dangling from his shoulder. The dew splattered our legs as Amelia and I ran after him. I pulled off my jacket, the sun already too warm. We were in the middle of what Tammy called "Indian Summer," which made me think of chiefs in feathered headdresses and squaws in beaded hides fanning themselves and drinking lemonade.

Calvin, the only person taller than Robert, covered a lot of ground quickly but stopped beside the first oak and waited for us to catch up. Amelia ran into his legs and encircled his waist with her arms. Panting, I stumbled beside them.

"Your mother's a lovely woman," Robert said.

He passed us, leading the way deeper into the woods. Amelia darted around his legs like a puppy while Calvin, taking up the rear, lit one of his hand-rolled cigarettes. I waited for Robert to tell Calvin to stop, but he didn't. The smell of cloves mixed with the scent of damp earth, decomposing leaves, and I wished it weren't there, so I could concentrate on what I was supposed to be smelling.

"She's a sweetheart," Calvin said. "Morning Glory."

"That's a flower," Amelia said.

I poked her in the ribs. "I know."

"The blossoms only open in the morning."

"Yeah, I know."

"She has high ideals," Robert said. "You should respect her for that."

I pushed my hair behind my ears, thinking about the braids. Tomorrow morning I'd ask Glory to do my hair before lessons. "Okay," I said.

Robert placed his hand on top of my head. "Good girl."

"Robert." Amelia hopped ahead down the path. "Where are we going to shoot?"

"Mi amour, you must have patience."

We walked for a very long time. When Amelia began to complain that her feet hurt, Robert playfully swatted at her legs with the bow.

"Will we see deer?" I said.

"Not if you girls keep on making so much noise."

"Robert and I once saw two deer making love," Amelia said.

From his place in the rear, Calvin let out his crow cackle.

"Breeding," Robert said. "What's a male deer called?"

"A buck."

"And a female deer?"

"A doe."

"And a baby deer?"

"Fawn."

Amelia rushed out the answers, but I knew them, too.

"Bucks have antlers for fighting," I said.

"And," Amelia said, "their antlers work as camouflage."

"Well done, girls."

"I've got one," Calvin said. "Who's the deer's worst enemy?"

"Man," Amelia and I said together.

We stopped in a small clearing farther into the woods than I had ever been. Amelia and I sat cross-legged in the grass while

Robert demonstrated how to stand with one foot forward, how to thread the bow. He shot at a tall maple. The arrow flew straight, pierced the trunk with ease. The tail of the arrow vibrated. Calvin put his fingers in his mouth and whistled, but Amelia was busy collecting leaves and twigs, forming a pile in her lap.

"Let me have a go," Calvin said.

His arrows fell short or went long. On his fourth try, he hit the tree, but low and to the left. When he tugged the arrow out of the trunk, the tip broke off.

"Shit." Calvin threw the broken arrow into the woods. "I used to be good at this."

"It's not life or death," Robert said.

Calvin handed the bow back to Robert and sat on his haunches, lit another cigarette. Amelia cast Calvin a sidelong glance, which ended with a knowing smile at me. I couldn't understand her crush. Calvin was too silly, too unpredictable, too much like a kid. And he stunk—of cloves, tobacco, and often body odor since he forgot about things like baths. Still I pretended to like Calvin, too, although not as much as Amelia did. She expected that from me, and there weren't many other options. Usually the men who came to Orion had wives or girlfriends, and their stays tended to be brief. Calvin had been there for two years, since we were six, a constant.

"Mi amour," Robert said, holding out his hand to Amelia.

She looked up from her nature project. She had started to braid the ends of the twigs and leaves together, forming one of her necklaces, which she would give to Calvin later. Carefully she set the chain down in the grass.

Robert knelt beside her and showed her how to hold the bow. I tried to make out his instructions, but he spoke too softly.

"Carrie," Calvin said. "Come over here. I've got a question for you."

I glared at him.

"Come on." When I didn't move, he began waving wildly. "Come on, Carrie. You're too far away. I can barely even see you."

I went to him but kept my attention on Robert and Amelia.

She tried to shoot, but the arrow popped out of the bow.

"What's Morning Glory's problem with me?" Calvin said.

"What problem?"

"That's what I'm asking you."

The arrow shot up high and came back down only a few feet away, landing close to a squirrel, which dropped its nut and scampered into the woods, bushy tail raised.

"Maybe you shouldn't call her Morning Glory," I said.

"She doesn't like that?"

"She thinks it's stupid."

Amelia spun around and pointed the bow at us.

"Whoa," Calvin said, putting up his hands in mock surrender.

Robert yanked Amelia's arm down.

"Never at a person," he said.

Amelia ground her toe into the dirt. "I was just pretending," she said, ducking her head so Robert couldn't see her grinning at me.

"Not even as pretend."

"Fine," Calvin said. "No more Morning Glory." He squinted at the end of his cigarette. "It was intended as a term of endearment, you know."

"It's too much," I said.

"What else?"

"You talk a lot during meetings."

"I have a lot to say. I believe in the power of the people."

"Yeah, but she says you go on and on."

"She's quite the fascist," Calvin said, "isn't Morning Glory?"

I shrugged. Amelia skipped back to her necklace, and Robert turned to me, his arm open to welcome me in.

What I remember most vividly about that afternoon is Robert's physical presence; he surrounded me, and as I sunk back into him, I found that I could float. This feeling, I realized, was what I'd been missing, the source of the jealousy that would twinge when I'd see Robert and Amelia on their porch, her sitting between his legs, leaning back against his stomach, his fingers combing through her hair. For all the times we'd played together, for all that he'd taught me, he'd never taken my body to him with such care and intention. No one had. Now, kneeling beside me, he moved my legs, straightening my knees into the proper stance. "Strong," he whispered into my ear, and my muscles tightened. I became a warrior, a stone statue. He maneuvered the bow, his hands my hands. My arrow sailed through the air in a perfect arc, stabbing the ground a foot in front of the tree.

"Well done," Robert said, as if I had hit the target, and I threw my arms around his neck, buried my face against his scratchy cheek. His hands on the small of my back pressed me closer. "That's my girl."

"Can I try again?"

"Of course."

I didn't hit the tree, but my arrows flew beautifully, catching the sun before falling back to the earth. Eventually Robert stood, and I realized that he and I were alone. The sun had grown higher; sweat slid down my back.

"Lunchtime," Robert said. "We better get back to Home."

I gathered the arrows. He lifted the quiver and slung it over my shoulder. The leather slapped against the back of my thigh as we walked. Robert took my hand and swung it as we made our way through the woods. He hummed a song that sounded familiar, something from a tape that often played at Home. Deep in the woods, I liked that I was the only one to hear it.

"Robert," I said.

He stopped humming. Several seconds passed, but he did not prod with questions.

"If things don't work out." I paused, not knowing exactly what to say, needing to get it right. "If Glory and Mike change their minds."

"They aren't happy?" he said and answered himself. "No, they're not."

"Can I stay here? With you?"

"Mi amour, you'll be fine."

"But can I stay?"

He tightened his grip on my hand.

"Yes," he said, "you can."

My heart leapt forward. I had to bite my lip to prevent myself from crying out.

We walked faster. Leaves crunched underfoot, lifting my already elevated mood. I spotted one of the birds Calvin carved out of wood, a blue jay, on the lower branches of an oak, its wings spread as if ready to take off.

"Carrie." Robert stopped. We were almost back; I could see the pond. "You shouldn't tell Glory and Mike about our conversation."

I had never intended to tell them.

"A child should be with her parents," he said, but the words lacked his usual sincerity.

"You don't believe that," I said. "Not always."

He was looking at the pond. I looked, too. The grasses sloped at an angle, ready to fall into the water.

"You're very perceptive," he said.

Perceptive was a word used to describe Amelia, not me. I glanced at his face to see if he was joking, but he looked serious.

"You remind me of Sara," he said.

There could be no greater compliment. I wanted to say thank you but somehow knew it would be wrong, so I brought his hand to my mouth and kissed his knuckles.

We didn't speak as we walked down the path toward Home, our silence deep and solemn, comforting, what had just passed between us remarkable, although neither of us understood the significance or consequences. All I knew that day was that Robert had promised to protect me; he'd claimed me as his own. Mike and Glory's arguments, their fits of passion, no longer mattered. Robert had made me his priority.

I reminded him of Sara.

By the time we reached Home, everyone had gathered around the dining table. I took my seat between Glory and Mike; Robert sat beside Amelia, her cheeks sunburned, her eyes tired. Calvin, next to Meg, who'd just moved by herself into Cabin B, wore Amelia's leaf and twig necklace.

Tammy brought out a pot of vegetable stew and began filling

our bowls. "How was the science lesson?" she asked.

"Highly productive," Robert said.

"Tell us what you learned, girls."

Amelia looked at Calvin, who adjusted his necklace.

"Physics," she said.

"Aerodynamics," Calvin added, and Amelia giggled.

Glory's face reddened. As she passed me a bowl, she held on to the rim a second too long. I felt the resistance and understood. That evening she talked to Robert for almost an hour beside the pond, and the next day in lessons Tammy lectured Amelia and me on the evils of violence. She showed us pictures from *National Geographic* of genocide in Africa. Amelia leaned forward, studying the bloodied faces. I pretended to look but aimed my eyes past the page, at Tammy's flowered skirt.

"A single act of violence," Tammy said, "can breed a hundred more."

Neither Amelia nor I confessed, and Tammy did not accuse, but she canceled our lessons and told us to spend the afternoon meditating on peace. Whenever I snuck a peek at Amelia, she had her back perfectly straight, her eyes closed, her palms on her thighs with her index fingers touching her thumbs. I longed to be able to sleep that way, too. I tried to quiet my mind, but it refused to cooperate. It kept traveling back to the woods, Robert, his rough hand covering mine, his hummed song, our secret.

I was like Sara.

By the time Tammy chimed the bell to lead us out of meditation, my back and legs felt numb. Amelia opened her eyes and smiled as if the day had just begun.

I don't know what words Tammy had with Robert, but for the next week he didn't have any free time. I saw him hauling dirt in the garden, scrubbing the floors in the kitchen, fixing the roofs on Home and Cabins A and C. He never took us shooting again.

✳

Glory and Mike's fights grew worse. She yelled at him for neglecting chores; he accused her of being Tammy's "minion."

"I thought this was a commune, not a cult."

"You can leave any time you want," she said. "You have free will."

"Free will. Now there's a joke."

Glory threw a mug. It hit the wall above Mike's head and shattered. For a moment the three of us held our breath, staring at the ceramic shards.

He walked out. She dropped to her knees.

"Help me," she said, and together we picked up the pieces. I cut my finger and sucked the blood away without her noticing.

Sometimes in the middle of the night I would get up for a drink of water and find Mike asleep on the floor next to the woodstove. And once, on the way to the outhouse, I saw him walking down the path with Meg, his arm around her waist, her head on his shoulder. I had to pee badly, but I intended to chase after them when I got out. I told myself that Meg was upset. Maybe she was sick, and Mike had come to the outhouse and found her throwing up. By the time I finished, they had disappeared.

The next morning, when I told Glory what I had seen, she burned her hand on the stove.

"Is Meg sick?" I asked as Glory crouched next to the water bucket, her hand submerged.

She stood, shaking her wrist. "Don't worry," she said. "Meg has never been better."

The oatmeal tasted like paste, but I ate it anyway.

five

THE TUG OF MY hair through their fingers.

A muscular thigh braced against a metal shelf.

My lipstick tube rolling across a scuffed black and white tile floor.

Their heads turning on pillows. Eyes opening.

Brown.

Hazel.

Blue.

WATCHING TV WITH MAYA and Peter, a fragment comes to me sharply and fades just as fast, the edges blurred, the sounds muffled, until I'm not even sure the memory is real. These fragments are loose and drifting, but not at all dreamlike; they lack any comfort, any longing to stay. I feel nothing, even though I know that in the moment there must have been passion, there must have been pleasure and fear and some sort of fulfillment. Otherwise, why would I be risking the very foundations of my life?

six

ONE OF US SHOT the squirrel, with perfect aim.

At the edge of the clearing it lay with eyes and mouth open, arms up, a scattering of acorns just out of reach, as if thrown. The arrow pierced the center of its chest. All afternoon Amelia and I had taken turns, passing the bow back and forth, at first aiming at the maple, then aiming anywhere. Long arcs, short arcs, straight up at the sky. We shot lying on our backs. We shot in yoga poses: Virabhadrasana I, Virabhadrasana II, through our legs in Downward Facing Dog. We shot with our eyes closed.

When the shadows lengthened, we knew it was time to go. Soon afternoon chores would be finished; the adults who worked off Orion would be returning; dinner prep would begin. The dangerous time of day approached, when the adults might pause, look beyond themselves, and wonder where the children were.

We'd last seen Robert hours ago, turning compost with Meg. Amelia had crawled beneath his bed and come out with the bow and arrows.

"A single act of violence," she'd said in a parody of Tammy's creaky voice, "can breed a hundred more."

She could always make me laugh.

Now we couldn't agree on how many arrows had been in the quiver. I said twelve; she said ten. We'd found nine, in trunks, low and high, mostly in the grass. I was thinking how lucky we were that none had broken when she let out a sound halfway between a gasp and a scream.

"We did this," she said.

She knelt and closed the squirrel's mouth with her finger.

"I didn't," I said.

"But it happened. We did it. No one else but us."

She took hold of the arrow.

"Don't," I said.

"We have to."

She braced her foot against the squirrel's side and pulled. The tip came away shiny with blood. She wiped it on the grass and slid it into the quiver with the others.

"Go ahead and cry," she said, but I didn't. Neither did she.

We dug a hole with our hands. Dirt wedged beneath our nails. We would scrub and scrub, but traces would cling to us for days. I'd find dirt in my hair, my underwear, between my toes. I'd taste it on my lips. It wasn't the same as the dirt from the vegetable garden or the mud of the pond. It tasted like death.

Amelia scooped up the squirrel and placed it in the grave. I was relieved to see that we had dug deep enough. We covered the squirrel over, stamped the ground, spread gold leaves.

"We're murderers," Amelia said, full of wonder.

"We didn't mean to do it."

"That doesn't matter. The end result is the same."

She took my hand, the dirt grainy, almost painful, between her skin and mine.

"Promise never to tell," she said. "Promise on Glory's life."

I promised.

For weeks we returned to that spot. We brought the brightest leaves as offerings and meditated, praying to Mother Nature for forgiveness. Sometimes I cried. Amelia kept her head bowed, her hair falling into her face, so I couldn't tell if her sniffles were from tears or the weather growing cold.

Snow came. By spring we couldn't tell where we had buried the squirrel, but we never forgot what we had done. Every time we looked into each other's eyes, the murder floated there, whole and gleaming.

Guilt can only hurt for so long if the cause goes undetected. Eventually our guilt over the squirrel loosened, lightened, the secret taking on the aura of mythology. Though we didn't speak of it, we both understood: the crime was one more thing that was ours, not theirs, and so it was to be treasured.

seven

"**You're a countess. You** live in a villa way up in the mountains, so high clouds press against the windows and the moon is close enough for you to borrow. You wear it as a brooch, pinned to the collar of your gowns, which are all rustling silk. You live on your own, but you aren't lonely. You have the creatures for company. You eat with the larks at breakfast, the sparrows at lunch, and the owls at dinner. Bats nest in your hair in the evening. You play the piano, and the notes bounce off the walls, turning into fireflies."

✳

"**You're an inventor.** You make a time machine out of pots and pans and old clock parts. No one believes it'll work, but it does. You travel back to the beginning of the universe. It's very dark and very hot, and you're afraid. Then there's a great flash, and it blinds you. It burns you. That's the start of it all. One moment, nothing exists, and the next, everything does. You come back to the present. Your sight is gone. Your face is scarred. People think you're mad, but what they think doesn't matter. They don't matter. You know what you witnessed, and you're thankful and proud because you accomplished what you set out to do."

✳

"You're Sara. You've left your body and returned to the earth. Your cells have become part of the dirt, the grass, the roots of the trees. You're the water moving up through the branches. You're the leaves beginning to bud. You're the birds in the trees, building nests. You're the baby birds with their mouths open, waiting for worms. You're the worms. You're the sun and the moon and the stars. You're me. You're the breath cycling through my lungs. You're the blood pumping through my veins. Here. Can you feel it? There you are."

✳

And I was, I was, I was.

eight

WE WATCH THE FIREWORKS, my husband, my daughter, and me. My daughter sits cross-legged in the grass, her upturned face bathed red and gold, while in the lawn chair next to me my husband crunches his water bottle and leans back, closes his eyes. I look at them and think: my family. This is my family.

But none of it seems real. Not the fireflies flashing out in the field, not the grass poking through my sandals, not the humidity sticking the plastic of the chair to my thighs. Most of all, not them.

I take my husband's hand.

"What?" he says, sitting up.

"Nothing," I tell him. "Just holding on."

nine

a dormouse set on escaping

the trap set

snapped

long before you were born

you do not want to mess with fairies who make their homes

in spiders' webs

the dew will drown you

before you've grown old enough for your eyes to

open

you

a kitten

mewing

stuffed into an old cotton sack

ten

IN THE PARKING LOT of my lover's apartment complex, Peter, my solid, stoic, scientific husband, is crying.

Beside me Eugene remains silent. He and I spent the last half hour making love, as we have been doing every Thursday for the past three weeks. Now we are on our way to get coffee, another ritual. He is the fourth man, the last, the only one who has stuck. We've been growing accustomed to each other, our bodies and simple pleasures, but when I am at home, I never think about him. That's why Peter's presence, the fact he has spent the last half hour sitting in his car, watching the door for us to emerge, strikes me as unfathomable. My mouth opens and nothing comes out.

Peter squints into Eugene's face, as if trying to recognize him.

I go to our car, open the passenger door, get inside. When Peter docs not join me, I turn around, expecting the men to have come to blows. But they just stand there, three feet apart, staring at each other.

Eugene turns away. Without a backward glance, he disappears into his building, as if he never existed, and I become just a woman sitting in a car, waiting for her husband to drive her home.

Peter's hands shake as he puts the key in the ignition.

"You've ruined everything," he says.

"Not everything."

I fold my hands in my lap and press my knuckles hard against my fingers, concentrating on the pressure.

"Our daughter," he says, and a sob closes his throat. He pulls over to the side of the road, drops his head onto the steering wheel. The horn sounds; we both jump. I try to arrange my expression so that I can give him the answer he wants, but he puts his head back down. I rub his shoulders until he's calmed down enough to drive.

At home the tears stop.

"What about the students?" I say.

"What students?" he says, his expression so open, so wounded, that I realize there have never been any young co-eds pressed against his desk, no jeans unbuttoned in the lab, mice squeaking in the background.

"Is that it?" he says. "Some sort of twisted revenge? For something that never even happened?"

I shake my head.

"Then why?"

The word repeats. Why, why, why.

Because Jeff's hands reminded me of Robert's. Because Eugene had Amelia's smile.

"I don't know," I say.

I'm telling the truth. I don't know. But I was going to stop. Eugene was going to be the last.

"We can repair this," I say.

On the sofa Peter sits with his head back, his arms hanging between his knees. "I waited out there like a fool," he says.

I kneel on the cushion beside him.

"I'll go," I say. "I'll go to California."

He turns his head, looks at me. "What makes you think I want you to come?"

Fall

one

I never became the seed

only the pod   split   into quarters

discarded next to the shed with

the broken down door

how much easier to have left me there for

the dogs to find and nash between their

teeth

two

SAMSON, THE RESCUE MOUSE, gets loose.

Maya crawls around the house, peeking under the sofa, lifting the rugs. I catch her leaving cheese in the corners of the kitchen.

"He's gone by now," I say, snatching the cheddar from her hands.

She sits on the floor in the middle of the room. "He's here," she says. "I know it."

"You're going to wait for him?"

She nods.

"And what? Grab him?"

"Yeah," she says flatly.

"Samson's fine. He's probably found a new group of mouse friends. I bet he's having the time of his life."

"You mean he's happier without me?"

Jesus.

"No, that's not what—no." I crouch next to her, put my arm around her shoulder. "But he's a mouse. Mice aren't meant to be confined."

"I still want to find him."

"Okay," I say. "But no more leaving cheese around the house."

✳

Without turning on the light, I take the Vicodin from the medicine cabinet. I shake the vial; only seven left. They were prescribed when I had two wisdom teeth pulled at the end of August, but the pain from the extraction couldn't compare to twisting in my stomach, the pinching at the back of my skull that has barely abated since Peter moved to California.

I've been rationing the pills for the worst moments. By the time I have an empty vial—before—I should be better.

After I swallow, I close my eyes and try to remember the way Amelia and I were taught to cycle our energy. I inhale deeply through my nose, exhale in one long rush through my mouth. My head grows light. I grab the counter to steady myself.

When I open my eyes, there is Samson, standing on his hind legs, twitching his fat cheeks, in the corner of the bathtub.

I lunge for him and slip, my hip and shoulder slamming into the side of the tub. He darts left, right, down the drain, my fingers clawing after him.

three

ON THANKSGIVING GLORY ARRIVES at nine o'clock in the morning with a turkey wrapped in aluminum foil and a pumpkin pie from the grocery store. I have never been able to cook meat that closely resembles the living animal, so I join Maya in front of the television. The Macy's parade is on. Maya lies on her stomach and watches celebrities whose names I don't know wave from floats that look like giant desserts and armies of handlers in stocking caps commandeer balloons the size of small airplanes.

"One time a balloon got loose," Maya says, "and knocked over a streetlight. Someone got killed."

"Where did you hear that?"

"A kid at school."

"That's not likely to happen."

She shrugs and kicks her feet in the air.

Glory comes in wiping her hands on a dishtowel. "All done with the slaughter," she says. "Is it too early to open a bottle of wine?"

"You shouldn't drink before noon," Maya says without looking away from the TV.

"It's a holiday," I say. "We're being festive."

Glory and I retreat to the kitchen. I open a chardonnay and begin chopping onions for the stuffing.

"What's gotten into Maya?" Glory says.

"Adolescence," I say, when what I really mean is Peter, me. I try again: "Her pet mouse got loose."

"Ugh. I never liked that thing."

Glory sits at the table and runs her finger along the rim of her glass. Her expression is drawn inward, but she sneaks me glances; I know that look—she's preparing to tell me something I won't want to hear.

"Have you talked to Amelia?" she says.

"Amelia?" I bring down the knife with force, making as much noise as possible against the cutting board. "Why would I have talked to her? We haven't been in touch for years. Decades. You know that."

"Robert called me," Glory says.

The knife slices into my finger. I watch as blood seeps to the surface, flowing in a thin stream onto the cutting board, ruining the onion. I put the knife down, turn on the faucet, and hold my finger beneath the lukewarm water. Then I remember that this is what you're supposed to do for burns. I put the cut to my mouth and suck.

"I'm bleeding," I say, holding out my injury to my mother.

She clucks her tongue against her teeth. "Band-Aids," she says.

"Bathroom."

She returns with a bright pink bandage, part of a pack of neon colors that Maya picked out. As she wraps my finger, she keeps making the tongue cluck, a sound I don't remember hearing from her before. She must have learned somewhere that tongue clucks are a grandmotherly cry of sympathy. "You should keep some first-aid stuff around the kitchen," she says.

"I have an aloe plant."

"That's not going to help when you're bleeding, is it?"

She settles back at the table. I sit across from her.

"Robert called," I say.

"I didn't know he had my number."

"Why did he?"

"He looked me up," Glory says. "On the internet. Gogol or whatever. Amazing, isn't it? You can find anyone these days." She snaps her fingers. "Just like that."

I get up. Utensils, cutting boards, vegetable debris litter the counter. I grab a sponge but don't know where to start.

"Amelia's missing," she says.

"What do you mean *missing?*"

"Robert got a letter from her a couple months ago. It worried him, so he tried to call her, but the number she'd given him had been disconnected."

I think about the postcard propped up against my alarm clock. It is the last thing I look at before falling asleep, the first thing I see when I wake up.

I almost say: she was here. She is here.

Instead, I say, "So? She probably changed her number and didn't tell him."

"He contacted the police," Glory says.

"That seems extreme."

"It's what I'd do."

I squeeze the sponge, digging my fingernails into my palm. Behind me Glory's chair creaks.

"They went to her apartment," she says. "The landlord was about to evict her. I guess she owed months of back rent. Her purse was gone, no one had seen her since August. You'd think that would be enough to file a missing persons report, but no. They think she just went off somewhere."

"She probably did."

"He is very distraught."

"So he called *you?* To help *him?*"

"I think he was just looking for someone who remembered. There aren't a lot of us left."

"I didn't even know he was still alive." I take out a trash bag and throw in the bloody onion. I throw the cutting board in, too, followed by the sponge. "He must be ancient."

"Late seventies," Glory says. "Could he be in his eighties?"

"What else did he say?"

"We only talked for a few minutes. It was awkward. I'm not good in those situations."

"Did you make the tongue cluck?"

"What?"

"Never mind."

Glory refills her wine glass. I am still holding the trash bag. I drop it and open the refrigerator, stare at the shelves. Today is Thanksgiving. I have a list of things that need to be done. I take out the cranberries in their plastic mold and plop them into a dish. From the living room come the brass and snare of a marching band playing "We Need a Little Christmas" against the wind, the notes muted, suddenly very loud.

"He asked about you," Glory says.

There we go.

I close my eyes to find the soothing darkness, but the kitchen light shines through my eyelids. I can't seem to gain control. Most of all I don't trust my hands. I trap them under my armpits.

"What did you tell him?"

"I said you were doing well. You're very happy." She holds her glass aloft, as if toasting herself. "I placed great emphasis on that point."

"I thought he would be dead."

"Sit down," Glory says.

I do. She retrieves my wine glass from the counter and places it in front of me. We drink solemnly, as if without this important step we cannot go on, which is probably true.

"Orion was bulldozed years ago," she says. "There's a subdevelopment there now. Two car garages. Landscaped hedges. Tammy must be spinning in her grave."

"Robert told you that?"

"I drive by sometimes. I've watched the changes." Glory waves away my surprise with her glass. "Oh, it's nothing, barely even out of the way."

"I couldn't do it," I say. "Even now, I couldn't do it."

"Life goes on, Carrie."

"What was in the letter?"

"He said it was like a suicide note. She'd tried before, you know. Three times."

I hate Glory's tone—that barely suppressed joy, relishing in someone else's misfortune.

"How would I know?" I say.

Glory frowns at her wine. "She's broken poor Robert's heart."

Poor Robert—something I never thought I'd hear Glory say.

I put my head down on the table, the wood cool, strange against my cheek. Funny, how this table, an object I use every day, could be so foreign. Glory pushes back her chair, and I worry that she will hug me. Instead she fills the sink with water and begins washing dishes.

"I'm sorry," Glory says. "I should have kept my mouth shut. It's Thanksgiving."

She opens the oven door. The smell of the turkey's burning flesh is unbearable, even with my nose pressed against the table.

"I'm going for a walk," I say.

Glory makes a noncommittal sound, preoccupied with the bird.

I slip upstairs to my bathroom and swallow the last two Vicodin pills. They lodge in my throat. I drink three glasses of water, trying to move them down, and pitch the empty vial into the trash. The orange stands out, too bright against the white tissues and cotton balls, a giveaway of my sins. I push it down, out of view.

The stench of burning flesh hangs over the downstairs hallway.

On my way out I poke my head into the living room. Maya hasn't moved.

"Do you need anything?" I ask. She shakes her head. On the screen a globular white kitten with an evil grin and big purple bow floats by.

"What is that?" I say. "It's menacing."

"It's just a cartoon," Maya says.

The ground is soggy, the sky gray, threatening snow. Next door at the Bergens' four cars crowd the driveway at odd angles. Smoke curls from the chimney, a wreath of dried leaves and acorns hangs on the door. This year I took the box of Thanksgiving decorations up from the basement and left it in the living room until Maya opened it and began taping construction paper turkeys to the walls.

"Thanksgiving was the day we murdered the Indians," she said.

"No," I told her. "It's when we had a big dinner with them to celebrate our friendship." But my facts sounded wrong.

"We gave them contaminated blankets," she said. I decided to let that one go. I watched as she placed blue ears of corn around a wicker cornucopia. "We need a little pumpkin."

"Sure," I said, but forgot to buy one.

I stick to the gravel berm of the road. From the houses comes the clatter of silverware, the uneven pulse of voices, the crying of a baby. Underneath my feet loose gravel goes flying. The road has no traffic, and combined with the low clouds, the effect is apocalyptic.

A suicide note.

Amelia must have been throwing him off, writing her own conclusion. I know she isn't dead. She is coming for me. The address tucked into my wallet could mean nothing else.

I take out my cell phone and call Peter.

"Is Maya okay?" he says.

I am annoying him, unnerving him: we don't call just to chat.

"She's fine," I say. "She's watching the parade."

As I turn down Ridgewood, a truck flies past, the driver laying on the horn.

"Where are you?" Peter says.

"I'm taking a walk. What are you doing today?"

"Working."

"On Thanksgiving?"

"I have nothing else to do."

"Why don't you go to Mark's?"

"He's out of town."

"Glory's over," I say. "She brought a turkey."

Peter doesn't respond. I stop walking, dizzy, the wine swarming around my stomach. A few houses down a Doberman slams against a chain link fence.

"Robert called her," I say.

I hold my phone away, check the reception.

"Peter?"

"Why?" he says.

"I'm not sure."

"Has he called you?"

"I think she put him off the idea."

"Have you thought about what you'll do if he does?"

"No. I don't know. Nothing."

This conversation is not going the way I intended. I cross the street to avoid the furiously barking dog. The fence looks barely tall enough to contain it.

"Maya's excited to see you at Christmas," I say. "That's still good for you, right?"

"Of course."

"She misses you."

"Leaving wasn't solely my decision."

"Going to California was."

"We need to talk about that," Peter says.

I have reached the end of Ridgewood and have a choice to turn toward town or circle back toward home. I choose town.

"About what?" I say.

"The next steps. How often I see Maya."

"You see her often enough, considering you're in California and she's in Ohio."

"You'll be getting a letter from my lawyer."

"Not now, Peter."

"Have a good Thanksgiving."

"Wait. Don't go."

I cross the railroad tracks and begin climbing up the hill toward the old center of town. The few remaining shops are closed. The white gazebo in the circle looks faded, a time traveler worse for the wear.

"Do you remember that apartment," I say, "above the carriage house?" My tongue feels heavy, cumbersome. I stop walking and take a deep breath, try to parse out my words. "The heat never worked right. We had that ratty flowered sofa, and we were happy. Idiotically happy."

My heartbeat thuds in my ears. I place my hand on my chest as if my touch could still it.

"Carrie," Peter says, "don't do this."

I snap my phone shut. At the top of the hill the 7-Eleven is lit up, a beacon of hope. Inside, an obese young man slumps over the counter. He does not look up from his cellphone screen. I wander up and down the aisles, the air freezing, the lights so bright they hurt my eyes. The artificial pink and yellow of the snack cakes seem to pulsate; the orange of the cellophane-wrapped crackers glows. Christmas music emanates from the speakers, classic carols redone by contemporary singers, the result incomprehensible.

I pick up a two-pack of Twinkies. My fingers sink into their spongy surface; when I lift them, the indentation stays. I slip the pack inside my coat pocket.

"Happy turkey day," the clerk calls as I push my way out the door.

I head home. As the reality of my actions sinks in, I break into a run. I half expect to hear sirens, to see the clerk jogging after me with pistol cocked. But no one follows me. No one spies out from between the curtains of the houses. No one puts down the turkey baster and points an accusing finger.

Glory is in the kitchen mixing biscuit dough. "Nice walk?" she says.

"Fine." I pick up the wine bottle, empty, and notice another open beside the mixer.

"We've moved on to merlot," Glory says.

I pour myself a glass.

The parade has finished; now Maya is watching *Miracle on 34th Street*.

"Here." I hold out the Twinkies. "Foraged from the great outdoors."

She looks at the Twinkies and turns back to the TV. "Those things never disintegrate," she says. "In a thousand years, those will still exist, even if we're all destroyed by nuclear war."

"Is that so?"

"Think what all those chemicals do to your stomach."

"Something awful," I say.

I rip open the package and take a bite. As I chew, I realize that I don't remember ever eating a Twinkie before. I try to like the taste, even though the sticky sweetness makes my stomach twist, my head ache.

"Okay," Maya says. "I'll have one."

"I thought you didn't like them."

She holds out her hand.

"Just this once," I say, more for myself than her. "It's okay if we're bad just this once."

She pokes her finger into the cake and expertly extracts the cream.

four

FOUR TIMES A YEAR the commune cleansed. We began with Commando—scrubbing down Home until the floors and fixtures shone. That part was fun. Tammy turned up the stereo, Calvin brought out his handmade bongos, and beautiful Meg worked her belly dance moves while wielding the mop. We began after dinner and worked straight through until just before dawn. Then we all came together around the long, wooden dining table to eat freshly baked bread spread thick with strawberry preserves.

As we finished eating, Tammy stood and raised her mug of tea.

"You," she said, "are the ones who dared. By stepping out of the rat race, off the corporate ladder, around the shards of the glass ceiling, you became a rebel. A radical. To those out there, those slaves to SAS, you're crazy. No one in his right mind would give up everything he worked so hard for to come into the woods and live in poverty among strangers. But that's what you have done. Why?"

Looking around the table, she made eye contact with each one of us in turn, holding for a second longer than comfortable so we knew she saw deep into our souls.

"What are you seeking?" she asked. "What do you hope to achieve?"

She let the silence linger.

"Wholeness," she answered for us. "Purity. Peace. Who are you away from their poisons of body and mind? Who are you away from their tarnishing of the soul? You have set for yourselves a grave and beautiful task—freedom."

She bowed her head. "I salute you, and now I challenge you to push deeper. Rid yourself of your remaining materialistic impulses. Reject that which is false and fragmented. Embrace all that is truthful and healthful and whole."

We chewed. We swallowed.

"Are you ready to recommit yourselves to the greater good of the Earth?"

"Yes," we answered as we licked the jam from our fingers, the crumbs from our plates.

She led the way to the meeting room, where we sat on the floor in a circle, closed our eyes, and meditated. As the sun came up, we ate one more slice of bread, the last food we would eat for a week.

Amelia and I had our lessons suspended. The men and women with jobs off Orion called in sick or took vacation days. Only the most necessary chores were attended to. Instead we meditated, practiced yoga, went for long, solitary walks in the woods. We drank water, at first for thirst and then to quiet our growling stomachs. Three times a day, we drank big mugs of apple cider. We were only supposed to speak when absolutely required.

The first afternoon our heads grew light. We had trouble sleeping that night. By the third day we heard sounds that were not there. By the fourth, some of us were seeing sights. Tammy urged us to meditate on those visions, to divine their true meaning. (Once her dead son, Orion, had come to her during a fast and given her his forgiveness; "The most formative experience of my life," she said, "besides his birth and death.") Often on the fifth or sixth day, someone fainted; then a little bread was allowed. On the seventh night, we broke our fast with a light broth. The next day, rice. We had to ease back into normal function.

When our bodies grew too weak to do anything else, Amelia and I would lay down in our spot, the grassy area between the pond and the woods. We sprawled out, our hands next to each other but not touching. I listened to my breathing, my heartbeat, and wondered each time if this would be the week I died.

Such occasions triggered truths. When we were eleven, Amelia broke the afternoon stillness by telling me that Sara wasn't dead.

I turned my head to look at her. She was staring at the sky.

"What do you mean?" I asked.

"She lives in Chicago," Amelia said, her voice a soft, dry monotone, the way we all spoke at this point in the cleanse. "I saw her address. Robert has it on a scrap of paper in his wallet."

"Are you serious?"

"Why would I be making this up?"

"Why were you looking in his wallet?"

"That's not the point."

I bit my lip and concentrated on the tops of the trees, bending in a wind we barely felt down on the ground. Amelia shifted so that her back was to me. She did not speak for a long time.

"Chicago's not that far," she said.

"States away."

"A few hours, probably."

"What did Robert say?"

"I didn't tell him."

"Could be an old address."

"The paper looked old," Amelia said. "But that doesn't mean anything."

"Well loved," I said without thinking.

Amelia rolled onto her back and drew her knees to her chest. She stretched her arms overhead and moved them up and down, like the wings of snow angles. The grass flattened and slowly unfolded.

"Curiouser," Amelia said, "and curiouser."

Briefly, nausea and dizziness overwhelmed me; from the hunger, I knew, but the hunger and this conversation seemed one and the same, and I wanted both to stop, to be able to lie again in silence. I put my palm over my eyes to block out the sun and took three deep, steadying breaths.

"I'm sure he didn't mean any harm," I said.

"He lied."

"You don't know that. You don't know what the address means."

"Carrie." Amelia spoke my name so sharply, my hand dropped

away. She was kneeling next to me. "We're talking about my mother."

"Sorry," I said, but I couldn't think of Sara as an actual mother, as commonplace as Glory or Tammy or Meg. She existed in a different realm—a mythological creature, a forever child, like us but better, a performer of miracles. And a scrap of paper was just a scrap of paper. "What are you going to do?"

"Nothing. For now." Amelia plucked at the grass, gathering blades in her fist. "I just wanted you to know. In case."

"In case what?"

She held her fist over my face and opened. The blades of grass came raining down. I sat up fast, brushing the grass off my nose and chin. I laughed, but she didn't. Her head was turned toward her cabin. She seemed to be listening, but I could hear nothing but the wind in the trees and a slight ringing in my ears.

"Maybe I'll need her someday," Amelia said.

She lay back down, the conversation over. I lay down, too, and thought about what a living Sara would mean. If what Amelia said was true and Robert had the address in his wallet, it meant he had been lying to us. He had never mentioned Chicago; Sara had lived and died in the blue house, next to the empty field that she filled with flowers.

A living Sara would change everything.

That afternoon, when we roused ourselves from the grass and made our way back to Amelia's cabin, I could not stop looking at the shrine. Sara was not as beautiful as our stories would have led you to believe: her blue eyes were small and mean; her lips too full; her nose too pointed. In Amelia's face, Sara's features had been softened, the eyes made larger, the lips less cynical, an angelic quality that she would not lose as she grew older.

"You're more beautiful," I said.

Amelia handed me a mug—the sides lumpy and the handle cracked, not suitable for the shop in Peninsula—filled to the brim with apple cider.

"You really think so?" she said.

"No question."

"I have her eyes, but she's more beautiful than I'll ever be."

"You're already more—"

"She's majestic."

But I felt Amelia's body straighten, her chin lift.

"Sara's waiting for me," she said.

She took a long drink, peering at me over the rim of the mug. Her eyes wanted me to argue, so she could rise to the challenge. I wrapped my arm around her shoulders, pulling her hard against me. Apple cider sloshed onto our toes. Amelia nestled her head against my neck. We were so used to each other's bodies, sometimes we forgot where one ended and the other began.

✳

THAT EVENING I SAW Robert sitting on his porch, talking to Calvin, who was showing off his newest carving, a hawk. As Calvin walked away, Robert stretched out his legs and looked up at the sky. I followed his gaze to the stars, just beginning to come out.

When I looked back, he was looking at me. He lifted his hand high, and I returned the gesture, feeling as sick with guilt as if I had been the one to lift the scrap of paper from his wallet.

I didn't know who was telling the truth, whether Sara was alive or dead. I wanted her to be both, to be neither. I wanted to trust equally the two people I loved most in the world.

I couldn't fathom either one of them ever hurting me.

five

I N   T H E   W E E K S   T H A T followed Amelia began to talk in earnest about finding Sara. Over the course of a few days, she had outlined the plan. We would sneak out in the middle of the night. She would leave a note for Robert on Sara's shrine, slipped into the corner of the picture frame. This detail seemed cruel to me, but Amelia assured me that she was just being practical: every morning the first thing Robert did was look at Sara's photograph.

I would meet Amelia beside the pond, and we would walk as stealthily as deer out the gates. We didn't know where the nearest bus station was, but if we kept walking, we would find one or a person who could point us in the right direction. Maybe a car would stop, and we'd get inside. We would both sit in the back in case the driver turned out to be a serial killer. If he made a grab for one of us, the other would attack: hitting him across the head with her book bag, clawing, biting, kicking, screaming. When he let go, the other would join in. We would aim for the eyes and the scrotum, our goal to do as much damage as possible so that when we fled, he would not be able to chase after us.

"We'll have his blood underneath our fingernails," Amelia said, relishing our toughness.

If required we would walk all night. After traversing the Cuyahoga Valley hills, our thighs would burn and knees ache. We would be exhausted by the time we stumbled into the bus station and asked for two one-way tickets to Chicago. We'd have been saving up; Amelia would make up the difference with money pilfered from

Robert's wallet. He owed her, she reasoned, for keeping her mother away.

"We can save enough on our own," I said.

For the past year Tammy had been giving each of us a dollar every month, an amount large enough to teach us how to manage money but small enough to prevent us from becoming materialistic. Recently, on a trip to Salvation Army with Glory and Tammy to shop for summer clothes, I'd blown five dollars on books—*Anne of Green Gables*, *Anne of Avonlea*, and *Little Women*, all approved by Tammy—but I knew I could do better. Amelia had plenty saved; Robert never permitted her to leave Orion and so she never faced temptation.

"What about food?" she said. "Traveling is expensive, and we don't know Sara's financial situation. It's not like she'll be expecting us."

"You'd be stealing."

"Sharing," Amelia said.

On the bus we would sit near the front and hold our book bags in our laps, since everyone knows people on buses are shifty and can't be trusted. At rest stops we would take turns going to the bathroom and then eat the apples and biscuits we'd packed, drink water from our thermos. We would doze in and out.

Amelia hadn't been outside Orion since she was seven and had been taken to the hospital for a fever that wouldn't break. "Akron smelled," she said. "There was too much noise, too much everything."

"Chicago's going to be worse," I told her.

"That's a sacrifice I'm prepared to make."

"Everyone will be angry. They'll be looking for us."

"No, they won't. I'll have told Robert everything in the note."

We were sitting by the pond. Amelia put her toes in the water and kicked, sending a spray up into the air, but the movement was rote, lacking joy. We watched the droplets disappear in the sun.

"We are coming back?" I said.

"Worrywart." She kicked harder. Water splashed onto my skirt.

"There's nothing wrong with seeing the world," she said. "You shouldn't feel guilty for opening your eyes."

"Maybe when we're older."

"Why wait?" She glared at me. "You see your mother every day. Now I want to see mine."

Once we reached Chicago, what would we do? Here the plan lost its momentum. Too many variables remained. What if the address was wrong? What if Sara didn't want to see us? What if we went all that way only to be turned back? Even Amelia's imagination could not stretch that far, and so she got us on the bus but never off again. We were forever riding through the Midwest countryside, past fields of green corn and bright red barns, our book bags heavy in our laps.

Eventually she stopped talking about Chicago. She stopped talking about Sara at all.

✳

WHEN MAYA WAS SIX, I suggested Chicago for our summer vacation. We visited the Children's Museum, the Field Museum, the Art Institute, Wrigley Field. We strolled through the tree-lined streets of Hyde Park. Everywhere we went, I scanned the faces of women in older middle age for traces of Amelia. I looked up at apartment windows outlined in twinkling lights, lit by solitary lamps, with gauzy curtains, tapestries on the walls, and wondered if that could be the place. I didn't know the address; Amelia had never shown me the scrap of paper, a fact that had never seemed odd until then.

✳

IN MY FAVORITE VERSION of Sara's life, she is a sculptor in a sun-flooded studio, carving abstract women out of sandstone, all curves and spheres and softness. She wears billowy smocks in pastel colors, her blond hair long and loose, hennaed patterns across her toes. She has Amelia's face, the face of an angel, and she hums while she works.

✳

WHAT IF WE'D GONE through with the plan? Our absence would have been detected quickly, if not by Robert then by Glory. Orion would have gone in search on foot and by car, and after a few hours, Tammy would have called the police. An alert would have been issued for two eleven-year-old girls, and Amelia and I, conspicuous with our book bags and outdated clothes, never would have made it to the bus station.

But let's be realistic. We wouldn't have gotten even that far. The moment we stepped outside the gates, we would have lost our nerve and gone back inside. We weren't ready to break free.

Still, I have never been able to let go of the alternative ending. In another universe, Amelia and I get on the bus and ride side-by-side to Chicago. We step together onto the stained sidewalk, hold hands through the jostling crowd. We knock on Sara's door, and when she answers, she is the girl in the photograph only warmer, brighter, nothing but love behind her blue eyes.

Sara, our happy ending.

✳

THESE THINGS CANNOT BE debated: when Amelia and I lay in the grass behind the pond and looked up at the clouds, she always found the shapes of women. She traced them with her finger until I could see them, too. Bountiful women with full skirts and overflowing bosoms. They were the good mothers from storybooks, round and warm, wanting nothing more than to provide care and comfort.

Above us they drifted and slowly pulled apart.

When I was pregnant with Maya, I dreamt of those clouds. They made me lonely; I woke in need. I'd place a hand on my stomach to reassure myself of my own roundness. Sometimes I would wake Peter by placing his hand on my stomach, too. "Baby's kicking," I'd say, and he would become alert, push back the sheets, turn on the lamp, and wait hunched above me for movement.

six

BY THE TIME WE turned twelve, Sara had disappeared from our collective consciousness, although I still held her in my own and sensed that Amelia thought about her, too. Sara had become a private matter, and my private life and Amelia's were no longer the same. I didn't know why, but a shift had occurred, an almost imperceptible crack that I was afraid to examine for fear it would expand. Amelia grew quieter, her stories fewer and farther between until they stopped altogether. I didn't know how to pick up the slack.

"Let's pretend," I'd say, and Amelia would turn to me with glassy eyes.

"We're too old for that," she'd say, but I could tell that she *had* been pretending, her daydreams going places I was no longer allowed to visit. Sometimes while lying in our spot behind the pond or sitting on her porch, she would get up and walk into the woods without saying a word. An hour or so later she'd come back and lie next to me as if nothing had happened.

"I needed some alone time," she'd say when I asked.

"Can't you be alone with me?"

She lifted one shoulder, my question not even worthy of a full shrug.

I began to have a recurring nightmare of sinking into the pond mud. I screamed for Amelia; I could see the top of her blond head above the grasses. But she never came to my rescue. It was as if my voice made no sound. The ground took me in with a sickening gulp.

One day, toward the end of winter, when we'd spent yet another long, boring afternoon in the meeting room rereading books we knew by heart, I decided to be daring.

"What about Sara?" I said.

Amelia flipped slowly through a *National Geographic*, the green of the jungles almost iridescent. I wished we could fall into the photos and become tangled, cradled in those vines.

She kept flipping, but I could tell from the tight line of her mouth that she'd heard me.

"We could still do it, you know."

Even as the words left my mouth, I didn't believe them. I knew she wouldn't either, and I hated my weakness, my inevitable failure to be the girl Amelia needed me to be. To be Sara.

Amelia slapped the magazine shut.

"Sure, Carrie," she said. "Why don't you go right ahead?"

✳

THE SPRING WE WERE thirteen, Amelia asked Calvin to give her guitar lessons. Every evening after dinner cleanup, she would go over to his cabin and stay until after dark. I'd sit on his porch and listen as he played a series of notes, which she'd try to repeat. She was horrible, which meant she wasn't really trying. Eventually the guitar playing would give way to conversation, and although I couldn't make out what they were saying, the gentle rhythm of their voices left me sick with envy.

One night I dozed off. Amelia opened the door to find me sprawled across the steps.

"Little creeper," she said but not loud enough for Calvin to hear. She closed the door gently and pulled me to my feet, leading me to our spot.

"You can't do that," she said, grinning.

"It's not fair." I knew I sounded childish, but I was too groggy to think of a better defense.

"You're right," she said. "I haven't been good to you, have I?"

I wasn't sure whether this was an apology or not.

"Not really," I said.

She took my hand and pressed it against her chest. "Do you feel that?"

Her heart thumped as if we had just raced through the woods.

"If I tell you why," Amelia said, "you can't tell anyone."

"I wouldn't."

"But you've got to promise. Swear." She paused. "On Sara's life."

"Amelia—"

"Do it. On Sara's life."

"All right. I swear."

"He kisses me."

I leaned forward, pressing my hand harder against her chest. "Since when?"

"February, but he got scared Robert would find out. And I got scared. I don't know why. There's really nothing to it. We just had to think of some way to be alone. Now it's been two weeks, three days."

I tried to detect some difference in her face, her body. Maybe she did look a little older, more confident. She looked happy.

"What's it feel like?" I asked.

"I can't describe it. I don't even have the words."

I stuffed my hands in my pockets.

"You're mad," she said.

I shook my head.

"Jealous?"

"A little." But jealous wasn't the right word for the burning in the pit of my stomach. It was something closer to panic.

"Listen," Amelia said. "What if I tell you everything I do with him? Then it'll be like it's happening to you, too."

Now I saw what the difference was: kissing had made her even more beautiful.

"All right," I said.

"But you can't hang around outside his cabin anymore. If he sees you, he might stop."

"What should I do?"

"I don't know. Use your imagination."

Glory called my name.

"Good night," Amelia said. "Sleep tight."

"Are you going to dream of Calvin?"

"Maybe." As she walked away, she waved her fingers one at a time, a coy gesture that seemed practiced, not intended for me.

✳

THUS BEGAN MY SEXUAL education.

A week later he reached under her shirt and touched her breasts.

"He pinched them," she said, wrinkling her nose.

"Like how?"

"Like this."

She pinched the skin on top of my hand. It hurt.

"But it's kind of nice," she said, "after awhile."

✳

SHE STARTED COMING HOME later and later. I would go over to her cabin and find Robert sitting alone on the porch or in the kitchen, a block of wood in one hand and a penknife in the other. We sat together for hours. Sometimes we talked. Sometimes we didn't.

I kept thinking about that scrap of paper, but I'd be betraying Amelia if I brought it up. I asked if he missed Sara.

He was quiet for a moment. Then he said, "Every father builds the world around his daughter."

But that wasn't true. Mike's world and mine had almost nothing to do with each other.

"She used to keep me company," Robert said. "Just like this. It was just her and me for a long, long time. We'd sit out on the porch, and I'd whittle away and tell her stories. When she got a little older, she told them to me."

"That's where Amelia gets it."

"Guess so."

"I don't know any stories."

He held a piece of birch, the bark still on. He'd told me that he never knew what he was going to make until just before the moment when he did.

"You underestimate yourself," he said.

"But it's still nice, isn't it, sitting here with me?"

"The best."

He scratched his ear, the knife in his hand.

"You should be careful with that," I said.

"You're looking out for me, huh?"

Of course I was. I had my own secret: I dreamt about Robert's hands touching my body the way Calvin's hands touched Amelia.

"Will you make me something?" I asked.

"What would you like?"

"Anything."

He began scraping off the bark. "The problem with my girls," he said, "is they've always run a little wild. A bit like me."

"You're not wild," I said.

His knife paused, but he did not look up.

"You're a good girl," he said.

✳

THE NEXT NIGHT I leaned my head against his shoulder. I imagined I could hear his heart beating through the plaid fabric of his shirt.

"Cold?" he said.

I nodded. I'd dressed in a tank top I'd borrowed from Meg's laundry pile and a pair of denim shorts. Goosebumps decorated my arms.

He put down the block of wood, wrapped his arm around my waist. I leaned closer.

After a moment he placed his hand on my thigh.

His fingers, heavy. Beneath them my skin looked ready, a blank slate.

He gave my leg two quick pats and picked up the wood again. He began to hum.

I stared at the place where his hand had been. My skin looked different. I wanted his fingers back, to find out what he would make of me, but didn't know how to ask.

Above the pond, fireflies pulsed.

✳

He didn't touch me that way again. Sitting beside him, I held my breath. I pressed my leg against his, nestled my chin against his shoulder, placed my hand on his back and felt his vertebrae through his shirt.

He would sigh, shift on the step. Wood shavings fell over our toes.

Months passed. Calvin pulled up Amelia's skirt. She felt him through his jeans. She held him in her hand.

"Are you going to make love?" I asked.

She tossed her hair; she'd taken to wearing it loose, moving it around.

"I haven't decided yet," she said, and I hated her, for being able to decide.

✳

GLORY GRABBED MY ELBOW. Her fingers pinched around the bone, and I yelped and jumped out of range.

"Where have you been?" she said.

"You know where."

"It's late." She stomped to the back of the room and spun around. "Do you think you should be spending so much time with him?"

Mike's snoring rumbled through the cabin. That fall he had been fired from his teaching position for missing too many days for cleansing. He now spent most of his time sleeping or wandering the grounds in a state very much like sleep.

"Yes," I said, "I do."

"Well, I don't." Glory's hand fluttered like a lost bird. She caught it, brought it to her chest. "It's inappropriate."

"He's my friend."

"No, he's your friend's grandfather. And you're getting older, you're maturing."

"So?"

"People will talk, if they haven't started already."

"Who's going to talk? Tammy? Meg?" The names shot out like ammunition; I kept going. "Louis? What's-his-name, Eddie?"

Glory put her hand over her eyes. "You know, Carrie," she said. "You know."

I did know, and I hated her for guessing.

"If Amelia isn't there," Glory said, "you will come back here."

"What am I going to do here? Watch Mike sulk?"

"That's enough."

She started toward her bedroom, but I wasn't going to let this end. I stamped my foot.

"What kind of man do you think Robert is?" I shouted.

"He's a man," Glory said. "It's that simple."

I expected her to slam her bedroom door, but she didn't. She retreated quietly, her shoulders hunched, as if I was the one who'd won.

Maybe I had.

I went out to the porch and looked across the pond at Robert's cabin. I imagined him sitting in the darkness of the kitchen with the wood block in his hand. If I went over now, I would catch him off guard. I could kneel before him, take his chin in my hands, kiss him on the lips. I would kiss well, with all the pent up power of my love.

To my left I sensed movement. Amelia, coming down the path.

"Hey," I said, and she froze. She looked from one side to the other and motioned for me to follow her around the pond.

Safely in our spot, she grabbed my shoulders and, giggling, slumped onto me.

"I'm high," she said.

"High? Like on drugs?"

"Pot." She rocked against me, giggling harder. "Calvin smoked me up."

"Tammy's going to kill you."

"Tammy," Amelia said, "is a fascist." She was laughing now, fully, barely getting out the words. "Tammy is never going to know."

Her hair smelled wonderful, like the earth. I took a handful and held it to my nose.

"What's it like?" I asked.

"Fun," Amelia said, calming, her breath slowing. "We'll get you high sometime, but you've got to keep it a secret."

"Why can't Robert know?" I thought about all the secrets he'd kept from Tammy, that we'd kept together: the candy bracelets, shooting practice, his hand on my thigh. "He wouldn't tell Tammy."

"Are you serious? He'd be pissed."

Pissed wasn't her word; she must have learned it from Calvin.

"If we explained why we—"

"Forget it," she said. "We're just kids to him. He's going to be pissed anyway that I'm getting in so late. Calvin was playing his drums and we just sort of lost track of time. He is seriously talented, Carrie. Have you ever listened to him play?"

"Sure, he plays all the time."

"No," Amelia said. "Have you ever *really* listened?"

I guessed I hadn't.

"Let's look at the stars," Amelia said.

As we lay on our backs, the anger I'd felt toward Glory came back with added forced, aimed now at the wide open sky, the absurdly bright stars, the crescent of moon hanging, almost lost, between the trees.

"There's Orion," Amelia said.

She pointed, but I couldn't follow her tracing. I'd never been good at finding constellations, even that one, which Tammy had pointed out countless times. "The Hunter," Tammy called it, and we understood that she didn't mean a hunter of animals but an archetype. "Strong and noble." Looking up at those stars, she'd felt her son's first kicks.

"You can see those stars from anywhere in the world," Amelia said, parroting the woman she'd called a fascist minutes before.

"I'm tired," I said. "I'm going in."

"Wait." Amelia propped up on her elbows. "If you don't walk me back, I'm going to fall into the pond."

Outside her cabin, she kissed me on the cheek.

"Tell no one," she said.

She leaned hard against the railing, planting each foot squarely on the step before pulling herself up to the next one. I listened as she bumped through the cabin, waiting for Robert's voice, but nothing came. By now he must have been in bed. I pictured the white sheet, the blue wool blanket pulled up around his shoulders.

His hand on my thigh.

Did it mean what I wanted it to mean? Or was I just a kid to him—a little girl with a crush?

Back in the cabin Glory sat in meditation on the floor. I tried to slip past her, but she reached out and grabbed my hand.

"We can do better," she said.

She had her eyes closed.

"Look at Tammy," she said. "Look at how beautifully Tammy lives. We can be that way, too, if we just make more of an effort."

I watched Glory's lips part, her chest lift.

I went to the window.

The night was black, with no definition. Earth was tiny, Robert had taught us, just one of many planets in the solar system, innumerable bodies in the universe. We spun and spun, year after year, generation after generation, the same pattern. I imagined the Earth spinning off its axis, flying away into the depths of the unknown. We would be swallowed up by the darkness. How long would it take us here, on Orion, to notice?

Glory began to chant, a long "OM"—the sound that is made up of every other sound. From the window, looking out at the blank night, I added my voice to hers until we were one note.

✳

I GOT HIGH WITH Amelia and Calvin once.

In Calvin's bedroom, we sat on a dirty red and white Navajo rug and passed around a bong shaped like a caterpillar. I coughed whenever I took a hit. Calvin told a story about a woman named Amy who'd hitchhiked from Providence, Rhode Island, to San Francisco, but I couldn't distinguish whether Amy was his sister or a lover or just some girl he'd heard of. She had many adventures. In Pennsylvania she saved a child from being run over by a train; in West Virginia she met a man who'd lost both his arms in a mining accident and played the slide guitar with his toes; and in Iowa City she had to take a job as a stripper. Her stage name was Bunny Mimefield, and she wore bunny ears and a black and white bikini to start out, with her face painted white like a mime's.

"Why'd she have to strip?" I said. "She wasn't paying for the rides."

But Calvin and Amelia weren't listening. Their lips were pressed together as he breathed smoke into her mouth. When she sat back, smoke leaking from her nose, she wore the expression of a happy dragon.

✳

THE NEXT AFTERNOON I kissed Robert, right below Sara's shrine.

When he pushed me away, I looked up at her, into her small, mean eyes.

"Carrie," he said, but from the way he hung his head I knew I had not been mistaken—he did want me.

A few days later I tried again, and he kissed me back.

seven

"How old were you?" Peter said.

I picked up the champagne, but we'd finished the bottle—or I had, mostly, our second that night. A week before we'd gotten engaged, and the new sense of security made me giddy. Along with the champagne, it had loosened my tongue.

"Thirteen," I said. "Fourteen."

"You can't consent at fourteen."

"Says who?"

"The law."

"It was Orion. We were beholden only to ourselves."

"And they were okay with that?" Peter's voice rose. "Tammy and all of them? Amelia?"

"Of course not."

He crossed his legs, his thumb slapping his knee, his jeans riding up to show his socks, loud rainbow stripes with a hole on the ankle. I'd bought him the pair on a whim, intending to brighten up his wardrobe of black t-shirts, black turtlenecks, an occasional dark blue button-down. The fact that he wore the socks so often they had holes in them made me unreasonably happy, but looking at them now, I felt afraid. I wanted to take my secrets back.

"Did you have sex with him?"

"No," I said, twisting my engagement ring around my finger, not saying that I had wanted to, if he'd been willing.

"It ended in disaster," I said, an offering. "You shouldn't hold my past against me."

"I'm not. God, Carrie, you were a child. I would never blame you."

But he did. I felt his blame even as he put his arm around me and pulled me close. I was not what he had been expecting, not what he had signed up for.

"What did he do to you, exactly?" he said, stroking my hair.

"I don't remember."

That was the truth. I remembered the pain of the rejected kiss, the elation of the first received one. I remembered long afternoons in the woods with the sunlight obscuring his features, the earth hard against my back, the skin of his hands rough on my stomach, a place paler than the rest of my body and which struck me as unspeakably vulnerable, the most divine gift I could give him. I remembered talking, but I could not remember about what. I could not even remember the sound of his voice, although that, thankfully, came back to me later.

"They should have gone to the police," Peter said. "I can't believe your parents didn't—"

"They didn't know."

His fingers ran through my hair. Inside I screamed for his touch to stop. I scooted away, just an inch.

"Have you talked to anyone about it?" Peter said.

"Sure."

"I mean a professional."

"Yeah," I lied. "In college."

I picked up the empty bottles.

"Champagne headache," I said.

After I went to bed, I could hear Peter in the kitchen, washing up. He took a long time, and I understood what I had to do. It came down to self-preservation; if he knew the truth, he would stop loving me. And so, to save us, I reclaimed the role I knew best: the keeper of secrets.

December

one

I **WAKE TO THE** knocking of pipes, the hollow force of warmth being breathed into our home. I open my own lungs and reach my cold toes back to touch Peter's leg. I kick against empty space.

He's gone, and I know where—he's with that girl, that grad student, gazing up at him with her doe-eyed need for guidance, her back bent over the lab table, her lab coat falling from her shoulders.

My foot comes to rest on top of my shin. There is no knocking, only the silent depth of Sunday morning, the aftermath of the first snowfall of the season. Time is out of order.

I might be losing my mind.

The concern is abstract and falls away as I swing my legs over the side of the bed and look at Amelia's postcard.

"Good morning," I say.

Last night I turned on the porch light, and Maya and I stood inside the door and watched the snowflakes spin in the orange glow. She leaned against me, giddy with delight, wearing her flannel nightgown printed with penguins in Santa hats. One week remains before I have to put her on a plane to California. To be a good mother, I have started a packing list on the back of an index card. *Underwear*, I wrote, before abandoning the list on top of the papers from Peter's lawyer, buried now beneath unopened junk mail on the counter beside the refrigerator.

I use the sleeve of my bathrobe to wipe clear the glass above the kitchen sink. As I sip my tea, I gaze out at a backyard transformed.

Today I am forty years old.

On the table I find a card Maya has made for me, a sheet of pink construction paper folded in half, crayoned flowers (roses, maybe carnations or daises, jubilantly yellow) on the front, and inside *Happy Birthday*, every letter a different color. I prop the card up in the center of the table, thinking it might be my last one. Soon she will be too old to make me cards like this.

At Orion we marked birthdays with an extra hour of meditation after breakfast. I'll do the same today after I've sent Maya off to school. I'll call off work and spend the whole morning with my eyes closed.

Before we began, Tammy would tell us to reflect on our current state of being, to focus our intention.

I sit at the table with the pencil and pad we keep next to the telephone. Fat, wet snowflakes splatter against the window.

I write: *Me*
40
~~*Divorced*~~ *Separated*
Eh job
Homeowner
OK relationship with mother
Beautiful, gifted daughter
I draw a box around these words. The action feels important. I draw a larger box around that box, and then a third. I am being highly productive, doing the work of the mind, defining my boundaries. By the time Maya comes down for breakfast, I will have figured out my past, present, and future. I will be a better mother, a more deeply actualized woman.

Above the boxes, I write: *Where are you, Amelia?*

two

WE WERE IN LOVE for the first time. It happens to everyone. The crush on the teacher. The kiss from the boy down the block. Holding hands with Jackie Johnson at the movie theater. Taking your shirt off in the back of a car.

But Amelia and I, the only two children in the world, had limited options. We had each other, and we had Robert and Calvin and Mike and the ever-changing others whose names we forgot within days of their departure, if we bothered to learn them in the first place. Amelia chose Calvin. I chose Robert. Men we loved and trusted. Men who loved us.

What else were we to do? Never grow up?

✳

MAYA NO LONGER ALLOWS me into dressing rooms. This summer at the community pool, I noticed how she pulled at the straps of her bathing suit while waiting at the diving board, how she wrapped her arms around her chest and hugged herself tightly. Her discomfort made me sad for what's been lost already, fearful for what losses are to come. But I am a better mother than Glory. I have paid attention to my daughter, filled her up with confidence and self-worth, left her with no uncertainty of my love. At least that's what I have tried to do.

✳

When I said I wanted to make love, Robert looked up at the sky and shook his head. We were lying on our backs in the clearing where long ago he had taken Amelia and me for our shooting lesson. Somewhere to the right Amelia and I had buried the squirrel, and I kept glancing over, searching for a bump, but no telltale heart beat up through the earth, giving us away. Amelia and I had packed our secret up tight, just like Robert and I were packing ours.

"You should wait for someone more suitable," Robert said.

"Why not you?"

He laughed—at the time it seemed cruel, and now it seems even more so. "Mi amour," he said, "you're too young."

He had never seen me completely. Only bits and pieces. My shirt pulled up to reveal my breasts. My jeans pushed just below my hips.

The way his eyes watered, the way he stopped my hand, his fingers curled around my wrist, with a sharp intake of air, and moved me away from him with a little shove, revealed how much power I had over him. That power startled and excited me, like falling against a wall in a house you had lived in all your life and that wall giving way, opening into a new realm where the hills rolled away from you and the sky spread above endless and blue. I wanted to stay there, wandering deeper and deeper, exploring the boundaries forever. But if I reached for him again, he would sit up and straighten his clothes. When I nuzzled my head into his neck, he allowed me, but his posture remained stiff, as if he were doing me a courtesy. I felt sorry for myself, but not enough to give up hope that, one day, he would understand that his desire for me was nothing to be ashamed of. Then he would be able to open up and give himself to me fully. When that day came, I would be ready.

With Amelia and Calvin, the power flowed in the opposite direction. He did not fear her; he led, and she followed with the eagerness and gratitude of a lost puppy scooped up in a parking lot. Her love for him was soft and malleable while his for her was harder edged: he was training her to be his willing woman.

Part of me was jealous, another part disdainful. What Robert and I shared seemed so far above what Amelia had with Calvin, which struck me as juvenile and base. My love for Robert had no shape, no texture. I believed that it was as pure and thin and vital as the air.

Around that time Tammy gave us a history assignment: choose a heroic figure to research and write about. I chose Joan of Arc. Our resources were limited—the *Encyclopedia Britannica*, our outdated textbooks, a few dog-eared history and art books donated by members or picked up over the years from Salvation Army—but I found out all I needed to know about sacrificing yourself for that which was true and good. My favorite picture depicted Joan of Arc at the stake, her shackled arms lifted toward Heaven as red and orange flames licked at her breasts.

Society, Tammy had taught us, could be wrong, and when it was, breaking the rules became noble.

I thought about my silence over Robert, my silence over Amelia and Calvin. What we were doing was wrong in Tammy's eyes. She expected Amelia and me to be pure of body, mind, and soul, which meant staying children for years to come, maybe forever. It meant living the life her son never had. Without being given a choice, Amelia and I had had our own lives taken over, taken away. We had become symbols of Orion and nothing more.

If Tammy found out, if Mike and Glory found out, I didn't know the consequences, only that they would be terrible. But they were not the only ones I had to guard against. If Robert knew about Amelia and Calvin, he would demand that they stop; he would tell Tammy, because he thought of Amelia as his granddaughter, Calvin as his friend, not as two people with free will, in love. And if Amelia found out about Robert and me, she would be angry, at Robert, at me, because she saw him as her grandfather, me as the sidekick, always faithful, always waiting, incapable of having a story of my own.

I lived by myself in the truth. To protect the people I loved, I had to stay silent, vigilant, even if it meant being lonely. Even if it meant I had to be brave.

For them, I promised I would be strong.

The one thing I regretted was that with her golden hair and serene face, Joan of Arc looked more like Amelia—more like Sara—than like me.

three

AMELIA WALKED QUICKLY, ARMS swinging at her sides, head lifted as if scanning the horizon for someone waiting. All I saw were trees. I seldom came to the woods alone, and when I did, I got lost. Robert had tried to teach me the names of the trees, the plants, the birds. I could parrot them back to him, but by our next lesson, I'd have forgotten all but the most obvious: oak, pine, blue jay, cardinal.

It was late May, we were fourteen, and recently I had started thinking about the rest of my life. I'd overheard Glory fretting to Mike about colleges, how they might react to a home-school education.

"You should have started worrying about that before now," Mike said.

"I have not fucked up my daughter's life." From my position on the porch, I could picture Glory: lips pinched, arms folded, hands clawing her sides. "You have played as big a part in this as I have."

"If I thought we were setting her up for failure," Mike said, "don't you think I would have done something about it?"

When Glory didn't answer, he said, "Well, I would have."

That evening I'd asked Robert if he thought I was set up for failure.

"You'll be fine," he said. "You're smart and resourceful."

I added those words to my mental list of traits he'd given me, along with perceptive, thoughtful, adaptive, resilient, and beautiful. Often as I lay in bed or walked alone across the grounds, I mouthed the words. I tried to attach them to my thoughts and actions. When

I picked daffodils for Glory and put them in a glass jar on the windowsill, I called myself thoughtful. When I used clay from the pond to fill a mouse hole in my bedroom, I called myself adaptive and resourceful. Yet none of the words seemed to stick. They slipped off of me as soon as I'd finished attaching them, and the most slippery word of all was beautiful.

Few mirrors existed at Orion. We were not supposed to waste time on superficial concerns and vanity was the most superficial of all. But I knew where Glory hid the hand mirror her grandmother had given her, the one plated in silver that used to be part of a brush and comb set on her dressing table in the house we had before. She kept the mirror wrapped in tissue paper, tucked away on the closet shelf in her bedroom beneath a shoebox of my baby clothes she hadn't been able to make herself give away. Alone in the cabin, I took the mirror down and carefully unwrapped the tissue, which had become thin and torn in places. Looking into the glass, I wanted to see a woman, but I always saw a little girl.

My future was a great black expanse. Sometimes I found comfort there, the black reminiscent of the darkness of meditation, the unfathomable space beyond and within. More often the black indicated nothingness. I would exist in the future, that was a guarantee, but I had no idea how or why or what for.

I kept hoping Robert would tell me.

Amelia hoisted herself into a tree, climbing one row higher to straddle a fat branch.

"Come on," she said and hung down her hand to help me.

My palm sweated against hers, my shoes scraped the bark. I'd never been able to climb gracefully. As soon as I settled on the branch, vertigo overcame me, as it always did up in the trees.

"Breathe deeply," Amelia said. "You're being held by Mother Nature."

"Yes, Tammy."

"I mean it. You have to give calm to get calm." Amelia leaned back against the trunk and surveyed her domain. "In another life I was a sparrow," she said. "Or a squirrel."

Whenever Robert called me beautiful, I thought of Amelia. No one could deny her beauty. Even a grandfather had to note it, appreciate it, understand the way others compared to it. I was not jealous, exactly, but I wished beauty could be communal. Everyone was not equal, no matter what Tammy and the others preached.

"Calvin and I are going on a little trip," Amelia said.

She inspected her fingernails, which were embedded with dirt, just like mine. After lessons that morning we'd helped Tammy weed the vegetable garden.

"Where?"

"Not far. He knows this motel."

"A *motel*?"

Amelia's head jerked up. "Don't say it like that."

"For how long?"

"Just a couple days."

"If he has you to himself, why would he want to bring you back?"

"God, Carrie. He's not kidnapping me."

"They're not going to like it."

"No one's going to tell them."

"Don't you think they'll notice?"

"It's no big deal." She sat up straight, rubbing her back into the tree trunk. "We just need some time alone together to figure things out."

"Figure what out?"

"You know, future stuff. And when we get back, we'll explain it all to them. And if they don't like it, we'll leave."

"Leave Orion?"

"Yeah." She took down her ponytail, looping the rubber band around her wrist. "If we have to."

I didn't believe her. She would never leave me. From the way her eyes skirted mine, I knew she didn't believe herself.

"But he's so." I looked up through the branches, into the kaleidoscope of leaves, and my vertigo returned. To keep from falling, I tightened my thighs around the branch and focused on Amelia, who was squinting, her mouth puckered, ready to voice her objection. "Like he is," I said.

She blew out. "He really isn't all that bad. You don't know what he's like when we're alone."

I thought about Robert, his hands wrapped around my waist, his fingers meeting at the base of my spine. He made me feel simultaneously small and larger than life.

"When?" I said.

"Soon."

I peeled bark off the branch and let the pieces fall one by one to the ground. Amelia turned her head away. She whistled shrilly, and a bird answered back. She whistled again.

"Did Calvin teach you that?" I said.

"No, Robert. Hey, stop." She put her hand on my wrist. "That's not good for the tree."

She removed her hand and pressed her palms against her knees, readying herself for the real reason she'd brought me here.

"I'm going to make him take us there first," she said. "Like a preview."

"Why?"

"You know. That way you'll be able to picture where I am. You won't miss me so much."

But that wasn't the reason. I could sense her fear, and I understood. If I went with them and saw the motel room, she could go away with Calvin safe in the knowledge that I was still with her, she had not left me, she could always—would always—come back.

"I'm not sure I want to."

Her face tightened and went slack, as if I had struck her. "You won't come?"

"It's a stupid idea."

"So. You're not coming."

"Amelia," I said. "Think about what you're risking."

Risking. Speaking the word gave me a thrill. I leaned toward her, cruelty shooting hot through my body, radiating out into the bright afternoon.

She swung her leg over the side of the branch and jumped, landing with her knees bent and arms up like a gymnast. All my need to harm vanished. I scurried to reach the ground before she got too far ahead and ended up half-falling, half-skidding, scraping my arms, bloodying my palms.

She wasn't walking fast.

"All right," I said. "I'll go."

She hugged me. As I held her, the bird that she had whistled for let out three short calls, sending a chill down my spine. I had heard that bird often in these woods with Robert, but he had never taught me the call. He'd never even told me the bird's name.

✳

THE CAB OF CALVIN'S pickup smelled damp, as if the windows had been left open during a rainstorm. He drove along the rutted path with his left hand hooked through the bottom of the steering wheel and his right on Amelia's thigh. Although no one could see inside the cab, no one was even outside, Calvin's hand on Amelia's thigh seemed like a public announcement of their relationship. Later I would wonder if that was exactly what he'd been doing—announcing their relationship, to me—or if I only wanted to believe such a barrier existed and needed overcoming.

Amelia wore a short red sundress, pilled cotton, a hand-me-down from Meg. The shoulder straps sagged, but she had more cleavage than I had realized. When a strap slid down her shoulder, she pushed it back up with a glance at Calvin. Every movement, from crossing her legs to scratching her nose to leaning forward to look at the gates and craning back to watch them disappear, seemed intended for his attention.

I hadn't seen her in action before. Pressed against the window, my legs twisted around each other, my elbows pinned to my sides, I felt embarrassed for us both. I hoped I didn't appear to be trying so hard with Robert.

As we swung onto the freeway, Calvin turned up the radio, a bluegrass song with wheeling violins, stomping feet, a man with a gravely voice.

"Give me a smoke, sweets," he said, and Amelia took a silver case from the glove compartment and removed one of his hand-rolled cigarettes. She placed the cigarette between his lips but had trouble with the lighter, an ugly plastic thing.

"It's hurting my finger," she said.

Calvin lifted his hand from the wheel. The pickup drifted toward the center of the road, almost to the other side before he had the cigarette lit, opened his window, and took his first long drag. Despite the rush of air, the truck filled with the sweet, sticky scent of cloves.

"Those still give you cancer," I said.

Amelia knocked her foot against mine. She wore only sandals; I had on tennis shoes. I knocked back with enough force to bruise. I felt angry at myself for coming on this trip and angrier at her for asking me to. On an ordinary afternoon I would be in the woods with Robert, having my "science lesson." Today he would be at Home instead, drinking tea with Tammy, who would praise Calvin for volunteering to run errands and taking us with him. Amelia and I were growing up, Tammy would say. We needed to get off Orion more often, see more of the outside world so we would understand why we had been chosen for this life.

"They're good girls," she'd say and get that faraway look in her eye which meant she was thinking about her dead son. They would both get sad and silent for a while. At such moments I never knew how Robert thought of me: as his lover or as his child. When he reflected on what Tammy had lost, what he could lose, did he think of Amelia or me? Or Sara?

The pickup wobbled as we crested a hill, picked up speed on the way down. The sun came in hot through the windshield, and I regretted wearing jeans. I'd wanted to cover up, although I couldn't have explained why. To create a counterbalance, perhaps, to Amelia, who showed as much skin as she could get away with.

Calvin cleared this throat.

"Carrie," he said. "I want to thank you for coming out with us. I know it means a lot to Amelia."

I watched the trees break apart to become open fields. A blue sedan pulled alongside, two little boys bouncing around in the back, a woman with dark, shaggy hair driving, her hands at a perfect ten-and-two. A gold crucifix dangled from the rearview mirror.

"You may not approve," Calvin said, "but at least you're standing by your friend. I respect that. I really do."

"We're more like sisters," Amelia said, taking her shoulder strap between her thumb and forefinger and slowly lifting it up.

"It's good you two have had each other. Growing up in that place alone." He shook his head and flicked the stub of his cigarette out the window. "Now that would be trouble."

"If you don't like Orion," I said, "leave."

"I didn't say I didn't like Orion. Jesus, you can be harsh, you know that? You're as bad as your mother."

"You shouldn't throw things out the window."

"It's biodegradable."

"I find that highly unlikely."

"Hey," Amelia said. "Be nice, you two."

I turned my attention back out the window. The blue sedan had disappeared and we were alone again, shuddering past a wood frame barn, the roof caved in, a skinny horse in the field swishing its tail. To the left of the barn stood the burnt out remains of a house, and a little farther on a brown and white trailer. In the yard, a woman in denim shorts and a yellow halter top hung laundry on a line. She had a braid that reached her waist and swung like a pendulum as she twisted to pin up a sheet patterned in roses. The pickup rounded a curve, and trees surrounded us again. Through the branches I caught glimpses of houses, garages, the brightly colored plastic of swing sets.

This was life outside—real life—but I didn't see anything I wanted.

When the trees cleared, the highway divided, and Calvin pulled into a Sunoco station, got out to fill the tank.

Scooting into the driver's seat, Amelia stretched her arms overhead. She had shaved her armpits, the skin spotted with razor burn.

"Funny," Amelia said, "all of this is right outside."

I watched what she was watching: two teenage boys with skateboards and oversized t-shirts sharing a bottle of orange soda outside the gas station doors.

"I don't see anything remarkable," I said.

"Well, you go out more than me."

I did, but only when Glory badgered me to come with her and Tammy on a run to the McConnell farm or the thrift store. Tammy argued about prices, throwing out rhetoric about the sin of materialism, and Glory would blush and look at her shoes while I tried not to notice the way Lori and Jim McConnell or the middle-aged women in their Salvation Army smocks stared at us and then looked at each other.

Amelia slipped off her sandals and drew up her knees, resting her feet on the bottom of the steering wheel. "Robert likes keeping me prisoner," she said.

"He let you go this time."

"A fluke."

"He almost never leaves either. He just doesn't think of it."

She pointed to the boys. "Want to hear their story?"

Of course I did. "All right," I said.

"The little one's name is Elmer and the fat one is Clayton. They live with their Aunt Becky on a farm two miles south. She's old and losing her mind. She'll call them by their father's name, even though he's been dead ten years, and sometimes she leaves water boiling or the oven on or the bathtub running until water overflows and drips from the living room ceiling. She drives them crazy, but they can get away with anything. Right now they're skipping school. Neither one will admit that skipping school is boring. They can't stay at the farm, but everywhere interesting is too far away to get to on a skateboard. So they come up here and spend the money they stole from Aunt

Becky's purse on soda and candy bars and potato chips. If they see a pretty girl, they talk about her, but only after she leaves. They're too shy to flirt, especially in front of each other. Most of the time they don't talk at all. Like right now. They know each other far too well to have much to say. And they're not imaginative enough to make up stories."

Calvin opened the door. "Scoot, sweets," he said.

"Where's their mother?" I asked.

"Dead, too." Bracing her arms on the dashboard, Amelia swung her hips into the middle seat. "She was murdered by a serial killer, slit across the throat while walking the dog. Killed the dog, too. That was his fetish, women with dogs. They called him the Doberman Doer. But the brothers were too young to be deeply scarred. The little one, Elmer, he wants to be a doctor, but only in an abstract way. He faints at the sight of blood, which is ironic given his family's history. Maybe it's his mother's ghost haunting him from the inside out. He'll end up a long distance truck driver. And Clayton's going to be an accountant, which is weird because right now he hates math. He'll learn to love it because he has a crush on a girl who is really good with numbers. In fact, she cares about nothing else. Eventually they'll divorce, but not until they have five kids. Three boys and two girls. And a ferret named Pythagoras."

The pickup came to a sputtering start. "Who the hell are Elmer and Clayton?" Calvin said.

Amelia grinned at me. "Our exotic lovers."

She burrowed her face against my shoulder, and I looked over her head at Calvin, who fumbled to open the cigarette case, his lips pressed together, his eyes on the road.

Mosey Inn sat on a gravel lot next to a truck stop with a peeling billboard advertising the lunch special: a bacon cheeseburger, Coke, and tater tots for two-fifty. In the window of the motel office, a pink neon sign flashed Vacancies, and underneath By Hour, Day, or Week. Amelia and I waited outside while Calvin went in to get a room key. The afternoon had turned cloudy; far off thunder growled, as if warning us back. We pretended not to notice. Amelia rocked on her heels. The straps of her sundress slid down her shoulders, but she did not push them back up.

"This place looks like crap," she said.

The motel was long and narrow, two stories of beige aluminum siding and loose white trim. A faded plush Santa hung above the vacancy sign, his hands in the air as if begging for help, or admitting surrender. In the far corner of the lot a dented Cadillac idled, sending up plumes of exhaust.

"I bet there are bugs in the bed," Amelia said, "and mice in the walls."

"Better in the walls than in the room."

Amelia kicked at the gravel. "I wish you'd come with us."

"Where would I sleep?" I said. "In the bathtub?"

Through the wire mesh of the office window Calvin could be seen leaning on the counter, talking to a woman with big, red hair, like a clown's wig.

"We're going to make love," Amelia said.

She looked at me, her eyes wide with expectation, but why should I have any answers?

Why you, not me? I wanted to say. Why do you get to have everything?

"Don't you want to?"

She wiped her nose on her hand. "Yeah," she said. "Sure."

Calvin came out of the office holding up a key attached to a white plastic tag. "Room Five," he said. "I've paid for an hour."

The room was as small as my bedroom, the furnishings mismatched as if someone had tried to assemble the cheapest, most absurd arrangement possible: a twin bed covered in a water-stained green bedspread; a print of kittens in a wicker basket inside a plastic frame painted to look like wood; yellow drapes with orange tassels; peeling wallpaper stenciled with roosters; a single, bare light bulb.

"Be it ever so humble," Calvin said.

Amelia sat on the bed and put her face in her hands.

"Carrie." Calvin gestured at Amelia, but I stayed in the doorway.

I wasn't here to fight his battles.

Behind me the clouds broke. Rain hit the gravel, spraying my arms, the back of my neck.

"Sweets." Calvin knelt beside the bed and pulled Amelia's hands away from her face. She was not crying; in fact, her face registered no emotion. Her robot face. Calvin sat back on his heels, hands helplessly at his sides.

"Now I know where to picture you," I said.

She looked at me. "It's a hellhole."

"Sure, it is."

She laughed—forced, empty—and touched her temples. "My head hurts."

"You need food," Calvin said. He wrapped his arm around her waist and helped her up as if she were an invalid, or an old woman. She leaned her weight against him but kept her eyes on me.

"Wait here," Calvin said. "I'll get the truck."

He ran off into the rain.

"Second thoughts?" I said.

Amelia braced herself against the doorframe. "What would you do?"

I knew what I would do: I'd go wherever Robert took me. But Robert would never take me anywhere but into the woods.

I put my arm around Amelia, pressed my head against hers.

"I'm sorry," I said.

"For what?"

"Not liking him."

"He's not so bad," Amelia said, but she sounded tired.

She reached out her foot, caught water on her toes. The pickup groaned to a start. We watched as it nosed through the parking lot toward us.

At the truck stop, we each ordered a house salad, the only vegan item on the menu, the lettuce wilted, the tomato flavorless. Amelia pushed hers aside and opened a packet of saltines. We were the only customers except for two old men in Cleveland Indians caps at the counter, drinking coffee and smoking, trading jokes with the waitress whenever she came by. She was a large woman, manly but handsome, in a blue blouse and blue polyester slacks, a laminated button pinned to her breast showing two blond boys in baseball uniforms.

"Are those your sons?" Amelia asked.

"Grandsons." With a curved, manicured nail—peach, a gold sparkle at the tip—the waitress tapped each boy's face. "Matthew and Jason."

"How old are they?"

"Seven and nine."

She hovered at the end of our booth, but our questions had run out. Amelia and I were not used to conversations with strangers. We looked to Calvin for guidance. His head was bent over his salad.

"You sure you don't want something more?" the waitress said. "A burger or something?"

"We don't eat meat," Calvin said, without looking up.

"Right, you said. A biscuit then?"

"Or butter. Or milk. Or anything that comes from an animal." Calvin's voice rose. "We consider people who do barbaric."

"Barbaric?" Her fingers went to the button, patting the edges, covering the faces of her grandchildren. "That's a little harsh, don't you think?"

"I call it like I see it." Calvin threw down his plastic fork, and Amelia looked at me, her eyebrows raised—here we go.

"How would you like to be kept in a filthy metal pen," Calvin said, "with no room to turn around, never seeing the light of day? How'd you like to be injected with hormones and impregnated without giving consent or ever looking your mate in the eye? How'd you like to have your newborn baby taken away from you before you even have a chance to kiss it? And how'd you like to have your tits twisted and yanked by machines, the milk intended for your lost newborn stolen from you, too, so that someone, somewhere, could have a nice, fluffy buttermilk biscuit?"

The waitress took a step back, holding the coffeepot in front of her like a shield.

"Are you threatening me?" she said.

"No," Amelia said. "He's just telling you about factory farming."

Calvin grinned. "That's the truth, lady."

"Well," the waitress said. "I don't know. Everyone's entitled to their opinion, I guess."

"These aren't opinions," Calvin said, but she was already hurrying back to the counter. He shouted after her, "They're facts!"

"Was that necessary?" Amelia said.

"Sure." Calvin stabbed a chunk of tomato and held it up, examining it from every angle. "Seize the moment. Educate. Spread the word. We wouldn't be doing our Orion duty otherwise." He popped the tomato into his mouth. "Anyway, now she'll leave us alone."

"She was nice."

"Sure, she was nice. She wanted a big tip. That's the problem with everyone out here: they all have selfish motivations. You never know what you can believe."

"Cynic."

"I speak from experience, something you don't have."

"At least I'm not bitter."

"Ah youth," Calvin said. "Naïveté is bliss."

Amelia scooted down, folded her arms across her chest, and looked out at the flooding parking lot.

Sitting across from them, I had a flash of forward sight: Calvin and Amelia together five years from now, on a journey across the country, stopped for dinner. They would have been arguing for hours, for years, and the force of that argument would be what sustained them, an undercurrent of drama that kept them both feeling alive. Because they shared this need, they would be horrible and wonderful to each other, alternately pushing the other away and pulling close. They could love each other, I realized. Theirs was a future, defined, one that I could not have but something to fill the black space nonetheless.

"You have my blessing," I said.

They looked at me. The men at the bar laughed, momentarily

drowning out the radio—"Don't Come Around Here No More" by Tom Petty and the Heartbreakers.

Calvin rubbed his eyes. "Jesus," he said and folded his hands into a pyramid beneath his chin, as if he were praying.

✳

Two nights later, on the first night of a cleanse, they left. I was supposed to meet them outside Calvin's cabin, to see them off, but I stayed in bed and listened for the sound of the pickup's engine. When all I heard was the high-pitched pulse of crickets, I thought they had changed their minds. Without my presence Amelia had lost her nerve. My relief was almost like grief, unexpected and all-consuming, causing me to kick off the covers and start toward the door. Then I heard the far-off rumble, magnified by the night's stillness. I could feel the engine's vibrations running through the earth, up the floorboards, into my bare feet, even though such awareness was impossible, the pickup many yards away, already edging along the path, out the gates.

My stomach clenched as I pictured the yellow arcs of their headlights swinging over trees, across sleeping houses, briefly illuminating unknown faces. I thought about the deer creeping along the highway, captured in a blinding instant. Calvin would know how to miss them. Their thin legs would flail as they ran into the woods, their white tails disappearing last.

Amelia—who thought they would be gone only a few days, who believed this was just the first adventure along a series of adventures that would last the rest of her life—would be sitting up straight, peering through the windshield. She would be holding Calvin's hand, but she would not be thinking about him. Like me, she would be thinking about the cliff divers in the *National Geographic* that Tammy had shown us in our World Culture's lesson: the lithe brown bodies poised above a sheer drop, the water below roiling hungrily against the rocks.

"How do they survive?" Amelia had asked.

"Not all of them do," Tammy said. "That's what makes it so exciting."

I had given this excitement to Amelia. I had let her go so that she could have the adventure I could not.

Selfless, I thought. Saintly.

These words stuck.

Hours seemed to pass. I remained standing halfway between my bed and the door, waiting for what would happen next.

four

"IF YOU KNOW WHERE they are, you have to tell us."

I watched the shadows my feet made as I swung them.

Left, right. Left, right.

"You aren't helping anyone by keeping their secret."

At the dining table Robert leaned on his forearms and stared into a mug of hot water. Meg stood behind him, rubbing his shoulders, her long, straight hair falling across his back.

"Carrie," Tammy said. "Calvin is doing Amelia a grave harm by taking her away. If you don't tell us where they are, you'll be doing her a grave harm, too."

Against the back wall Glory remained as two-dimensional as a painting. Only her eyes moved, roaming the room, settling briefly on mine before rolling away again.

"I'm hungry," I said.

Tammy's expression was more pained than angry.

"If I had some food," I said, "maybe I could think better."

"A little bread," Glory said, barely a whisper.

Tammy loosened her folded arms. "The principles of this community must be abided by," she said. "Without principles, we have nothing. We might as well not exist."

"A special circumstance," Glory said.

Tammy looked toward the ceiling. After a moment, she nodded.

Glory went to the kitchen and came back with a chunk of bread, roughly torn off, which she placed in my hands. I watched, aware of everyone else watching, as my fingers plucked off a piece. I brought the piece to my lips, opened my mouth, and chewed, tasting nothing.

I wondered if saints were aware of human senses or if they had overcome them in favor of something better.

"We should notify the police," Tammy said.

"No." Robert looked up. "They're ours." His voice had a harder edge than I had ever heard in it. "Both of them."

Tammy sighed and rubbed her bony elbows as if from cold. My hand reached out to offer her the bread—a saintly gesture—before my mind intervened and pulled my hand back. Glory retook her position on the wall. She kept her head turned toward the meeting room, whether to express disgust at my deceit or support for my privacy, I wasn't sure. I looked toward the meeting room, too, but could not see inside to where Mike and the others sat with crossed legs and resting palms, listening.

The bread slipped from my hands onto the floor. Tammy looked at it. She began to stoop, then straightened and kicked the bread aside.

"Futile," Meg said. Her hands rested on Robert's chest. Seeing her hands there and Robert leaning back against her stomach, I felt a sharp pang of jealousy, the most intense emotion I had felt all morning—definitely not saintly. I grasped the edge of the stool to prevent myself from running to him.

At last, he looked at me.

"Mi amour," he said. "Why?"

I couldn't stand the exhaustion on his face. Tears welled up, distorting the room.

Robert stood. Meg's hands dropped. She clasped them in front of her and stepped back, demure and humble, her services no longer needed. I was glad to see her cast aside so easily.

"Walk with me," Robert said.

We went to the woods, but he didn't take my hand as we stepped behind the shelter of the trees, didn't smile down at me, didn't say my name or any of the numerous traits he'd bestowed upon me like medals, symbols of my uniqueness, my worthiness. He didn't answer the call of the birds or stop to name a tree or wildflower. He just walked with his head low and hands stuffed in the pockets of his jeans. I hurried to keep up, stumbling over tree roots, stubbing my toes on rocks.

My lips moved with all the things I could not say: They're at Mosey Inn, I had to let her go, I didn't want to but she would have done the same if she could have, if we could have, she would have wanted that for me.

But most of all: I'm sorry, I'm sorry, I'm sorry.

He led me to the clearing, where he squatted, wrapped his arms around his knees, and stared into the woods. The dappled light gave way to darkness, to destinations unknown, at least to me. I sat beside him and placed my hand on his back. Beneath my palm I could feel his unsteady breath.

"I'm very disappointed in you," he said.

"I love you," I said.

He turned away. I climbed my hand higher and pressed my fingers into his shirt until I could feel the outline of his spine.

"Did she leave because of us?" he said.

"She doesn't know."

"Are you certain?"

"She doesn't know."

He stretched out his legs and placed his hand lightly on my knee. His fingers lay inert, as if my knee held no significance, as if it merely happened to be the closest object on which to rest. I put my hand over his and lifted his fingers, threading them through mine. When I looked up, he was watching me.

"Are they safe?" he said.

"Yes."

"How far did they go?"

"Not far."

"Calvin isn't responsible. He skips jobs. We've had meetings about whether or not to expel him."

"Why weren't we at those meetings?"

Robert reached his free hand across my body and touched my cheek, his mouth inches away from mine. I examined the cracks in his lips. I licked my own.

"Mi amour," he said. "We have tried to protect you."

"From what?"

"The ugliness. The uncertainty. We wanted to give you the best childhood possible."

His hand fell away from my face, but I kept the other hand trapped.

"I have made many mistakes," he said. "I know that. But those mistakes are already made. They cannot be undone."

I didn't like his hopelessness. I brought his hand to my mouth and kissed his calloused fingers.

"No mistake," I said.

"Calvin and Amelia are not like us. You need to understand that. He is not responsible. She lacks maturity."

"Are you afraid she'll end up like Sara?"

"How perceptive," he said, the trait he valued in me most, but this time his eyes were hard.

My stomach rumbled, craving the bread I had dropped. Meanwhile Robert remained stoically silent, still.

Who was saintly now?

"I can take you there," I said.

Only I didn't remember exactly where we had driven in Calvin's pickup. Every turn-off looked the same. Robert drove slowly in Tammy's twenty-year-old sedan, his progress impeded by the hole in the back windshield covered by a black garbage bag, crisscrossed with duct tape. The wind sucked in through the plastic and made a horrible rushing sound, like being inside the vortex of a tornado. I had to shout my directions.

"There," I said as we drove past the Sunoco station. "I know that place."

Robert made a U-turn. He got out, leaving the car running, his door open. The radio was playing, a fact I had forgotten; the wind had drowned out the music. A man with a deep, smooth voice introduced a new Madonna song, the tempo upbeat and jaunty, dance club music, something Robert would think ridiculous. He liked Pete

Seeger, James Taylor, Joan Baez. I turned the radio off.

Robert returned with a sloppily folded map clutched to his chest.

"I'm sorry," I said.

He backed out of the parking space. "Don't worry, mi amour. We're on the right track now."

"No," I said. "About everything."

He wrapped his hand around the back of my neck. His skin felt cool. I pressed into his palm, hoping he had forgiven me and Amelia would forgive me, too.

We found the motel without any more trouble. As we pulled into the parking lot, Robert's jaw remained clenched.

"You're sure?" he said.

"Yes." I wished I could answer differently. "This is the place."

"I don't see Calvin's truck."

"Maybe they went to get food."

"Carrie," Robert said and looked as if he might cry.

I got out of the car and began walking toward the office. Behind me I heard the car door slam, his feet on the gravel. I stopped but did not turn to watch his approach. If I did, I understood that I would see Amelia's worried grandfather, not my lover, not the man I wanted to call my own. For now at least, I had to hold on to the little I still possessed.

Robert passed me and held the office door open. Behind the counter sat the woman with clown hair, painting her fingernails with clear polish, her lips pressed together in concentration.

"Good afternoon," Robert said.

She applied two more strokes to her pinkie, recapped the polish, blew on her fingers.

"By hour or by day," she said.

"I'm looking for my granddaughter," Robert said. "I believe she checked in here last night. Fourteen, blond, slight. She was with a man in his late thirties. He has long, curly hair."

"We don't check IDs," the woman said.

"Understood."

"He might have been her father. We don't get into our guests' business. That's not what we're here for."

"Understood," Robert said again. "Please, which room is she in?"

"I didn't give you a yes or a no."

Robert leaned on the counter and smiled his courtly smile, the one he used so effectively to defuse conflicts at Home. "I'm sure you can recognize how important it is for me to find her," he said.

"Well." The woman opened a three-ring binder and quickly closed it. She twisted the cap off her nail polish. "Room Nine. But you didn't hear that from me."

I was disappointed that their room was not the one we had visited together. I would have expected Amelia to be insistent, to demand that she sleep in the room that I had approved. The drapes of Room Nine, I noticed from the outside, were dusty pink, not yellow and orange.

He knocked on the door.

We waited.

"Maybe they're in the bathroom," I said.

Robert put his ear to the door. "No one's in there."

"Knock again."

He shook his head. "No one's home."

I stepped in front of him and slapped the door with my palm. Robert grabbed my shoulders and pushed me away. Without a word he turned and walked toward the car. I took another look at the drapes and followed.

I expected us to wait, but Robert started the engine.

"We'll come back later," I said.

He didn't answer.

"They wouldn't have gone far. We can drive around. Look for his truck."

Robert punched the steering wheel. I jumped, banging my arm against the door.

"Where?" he said. "Where the hell are we supposed to look?"

"I don't know."

"Then don't pretend like you do."

He pulled out of the parking lot so fast, the tires squealed.

On the highway, he said, "I'm sorry."

"It's all right."

"No, you shouldn't have had to witness that. I should have better self-control. It's a moral failing on my part."

I drew my knees to my chest.

"Put your legs down," he said.

"Why?"

"If the car crashes, you'll knee yourself in the neck. You'll damage your windpipe."

"That won't happen," I said, but I put my legs down and fastened my seatbelt.

We drove the rest of the way without speaking. I was grateful for the sound of the wind, the flapping plastic, making my thoughts inaudible.

Down the road from Orion, Robert pulled over and kissed me. He reached under my shirt and grabbed my breasts with none of his usual tenderness. He let go and fell against the steering wheel, breathing hard.

I reached for him but didn't know where to lay my hand. Every part of his body seemed wrong.

He straightened his shirt collar. "Mi amour," he said, but his voice sounded phlegmy, forced. He coughed. "That has to be it for a while."

"How long?"

"I'm not sure."

"You're punishing me."

"I'm protecting you," he said.

In the tall grasses by the side of the road, bees buzzed. Clover grew in a clump beside a bedraggled jack-in-the-pulpit, a sluggish bleeding heart.

"Forever?" I said.

He didn't answer; I don't think he heard me.

As we drove inside the gates, he said, "Not another word about it, mi amour."

five

HERE IS WHAT I imagined:

Amelia's body, almost luminescent in the dimness, stretched out on top of the green bedspread. She turns her head to watch as Calvin closes the drapes, walks to the bathroom, switches off the light. Beneath her the mattress sags, the pillows smell of mildew and stale perfumes, yet in the darkness the room takes on the coziness of Home. She closes her eyes and listens as Calvin bumps into the nightstand, mutters a curse. She reaches up her arms. She does not require sight. Already she understands the fluctuations of his body, the spicy scent of his skin, the murmur he makes low in his throat, as if calling to him a frightened animal. But she is not frightened. She has lived this moment before, the most profound of premonitions, holding it close in the quiet of her cabin bedroom, allowing it, not him, to transform her. She is never not in control.

※

HERE IS WHAT HAPPENED:

They stayed away five days.

In the early evening Calvin dropped her off at the gates and sped away in his pickup, never to be seen again. She had Band-Aids on her wrists and knots in her hair. She would not speak to anyone, not even me.

six

Now that I had her back—now that I had sacrificed all I had for her—I was never going to let her go.

Wherever she went, I followed, just as I had when we were little girls, only now she did not wait for me, she did not take my hand and lead. I trailed her like a shadow. Or a ghost.

Our lessons at Home were suspended indefinitely, and our days opened out before us empty and opaque. Amelia took to the woods. She climbed trees, and I sat at the base, peering up through the leaves at her swinging foot, her elbow poking through. Sometimes she looked down, and our eyes met. "Hello," I'd say, and she'd jerk back, climb higher, but never out of view.

Even in her silence, I knew she did not hate me. I wasn't so sure about Robert. He avoided me in the kitchen, would say only perfunctory things in the dining room. In the evening I saw him sitting on his porch, but I resisted going to him. I knew he would send me away—for my protection, he would say, but more so for his. He had promised that he would never leave me, and yet there I was, unceremoniously left.

* * *

One morning, a few days after Amelia returned, I woke to find Glory sitting on my bed. She placed her hand on my forehead as if checking for a fever then slid her hand down to cover my eyes.

"What are you doing?" I said.

"Shh. Go back to sleep."

"I can't with you here."

She pulled back the blanket and climbed into bed beside me. I turned my back to her, but she rested her cheek on my shoulder, wrapped her arms around me and interlocked her fingers, the heels of her hands pressing on my stomach, straining my bladder.

"My child," she whispered.

"You're scaring me."

"I know. I know." She withdrew her arms and sat up. "I have not been the best mother," she said.

I inched closer to the wall, made my body as small as possible, and held still, hoping she would think I'd fallen back asleep.

"Mike wants to leave," she said.

I stared at the wall. Sometimes at night I would knock into the logs, and in the morning I would find splinters in my arms and knees. In the winter the cold wind leaked through, and I shivered no matter how many blankets I burrowed underneath.

"Carrie," Glory said, "did you hear me?"

"With us?"

She shifted, pulling the covers away. "You don't want to leave, do you?"

"No."

"Because of Amelia. You two. Peas in a pod."

I reached behind me, found the blanket, and yanked it back over my shoulders.

"Has she told you what happened?" Glory said.

I didn't answer. I wasn't sure who was asking, Glory or Tammy. Either way I wouldn't betray Amelia's confidence—if she had confided in me.

"Don't worry," Glory said. "She will. In time."

"If Tammy calls the police, Amelia will hate her forever."

"The police? We have nothing to tell them."

"But Tammy—"

"What can Tammy do? She's as helpless as any of us." I felt the mattress rise as Glory got out of bed. "We're all ashamed," she said. "We failed to protect our child."

I rolled over and looked at her. She stood in her summer nightgown, her hair in disarray. The morning sun coming through the east window emphasized the wrinkles around her eyes and mouth, the new strands of gray at her scalp. I remembered that I used to think her pretty. Now she just looked old and afraid.

"I think we have something more to gain here," she said, "but Mike will leave anyway. He's been humoring me far too long."

Her matter-of-fact tone unnerved me more than the words she was saying. Mike had become increasingly withdrawn since losing his teaching job. I would see him laughing with Meg in the Home kitchen or talking with Eddie in the garden, but if Mike was in the cabin, he was in the bedroom with the door closed. I hadn't particularly missed him, but now I thought about those long ago Sunday afternoon excursions, the snuck hot dogs and sodas, the expression of bliss on his face as he bit into that cream filled doughnut. I'd gotten more joy out of watching him eat than from eating the doughnut myself.

As if reading my mind, Glory smiled and said, "When you were young, you were such a daddy's girl."

She went out, leaving my bedroom door open. I listened as she moved around the cabin. The kettle clanged on top of the stove; a window banged shut. She made no more noise than usual, yet every sound seemed to reverberate, proclaiming something to me. I wished I knew what.

✳

A WEEK INTO HER silence, Amelia turned and grabbed my wrist, her thumb directly over my pulse. "You wouldn't have wanted to be me," she said, her breath hot, foul-smelling, her fingernails split.

Without thinking, I said, "I am you."

She dug her thumbnail into my skin.

"Liar," she said, but in that moment I sensed she saw me more clearly than she ever had before.

I wanted to say, "I know what being in love is like. I know how much it hurts."

Instead I said, "You're the one who's been lying."

I sat down in the middle of the woods, on the path worn away by countless commune members' footsteps. She hesitated, toying with the ends of the Band-Aids.

"I haven't lied," she said. "I just haven't had the words."

"Pretend," I said. "You be you, and I'll be me."

"Does it work that way?"

"I don't know."

Her eyes went past me, to the woods.

"They go on forever," I said.

She blinked. "What do?"

"The trees. We can't outrun them."

"I'll tell you," she said, sitting down.

✳

ON THE WAY TO the motel, Amelia had picked a fight, accusing Calvin of not really loving her. She had delighted in the way he responded—hurt and outrage giving way to self-righteousness. "Would I be risking everything," he asked, "if I didn't love you?"

"Sex is a good motivator," she said, and he spat back, "I've had sex before, sweets. Sex means nothing."

"With Meg?"

He tossed his cigarette, not yet half gone, out the window. "I'm not going to answer that," he said.

"Meg's a slut."

"Meg's a good woman."

Amelia put her feet in Calvin's lap. He hated when she did that while he drove, but this time he grabbed her toes and held them.

"What am I?" Amelia said.

"A nympho." Calvin grinned, his tobacco-stained teeth shining in the headlights of an oncoming car. "A wood nymph set out to trick mortal man."

He'd given her the right answer.

That first night, while he was in the bathroom, she took off her clothes and lay in wait for him. When he came out, he didn't say a word, just stripped and stood over the bed. Unhurried, they looked at each other, absorbing the details for the first time. She felt disappointed. Calvin's body was not beautiful. His ribs were too prominent, reminding her of pictures of Jesus on the cross, and his stomach bulged as if he were pregnant. His penis hung limp. She decided to forgive him. Love transforms, and so she closed her eyes and took him in her hands.

The next morning was better. Instead of concentrating on his body, she focused on the look of adoration in his eyes.

But that afternoon, when they drove into town to get groceries, she caught him staring at the checkout girl's breasts. They were larger than Amelia's, cradled in an orange spandex top. "Find everything you were looking for?" the girl asked, and Calvin replied, "Oh, yes."

Why not just "yes"? Why did he have to add the "oh"?

Amelia did not speak to him on the drive back to the motel. He gave up asking her why. He sat on the floor and ate green grapes while she lay in bed with the blanket pulled over her head. Every once in a while he would throw a grape at her. She began to think the trip had been a mistake.

That night he came to bed stinking of cigarette smoke and sweat.

"Take a shower," she said, but he rolled on top of her. "Not now," she said and pushed against his shoulders. He got out of bed and paced the room. Then he took a baggie and the caterpillar bong out of his backpack and went into the bathroom. She resisted for several minutes before joining him. Without speaking they sat in the bathtub and smoked.

When they went back to bed, he made love to her, slowly and sweetly, with all the romance she had been waiting for.

The second and third days were blissful. On the fourth Amelia grew bored with sex.

"We haven't talked about the future yet," she said.

Calvin flipped through TV channels. On a garishly lit stage three overweight teenage girls sat on folding chairs and screamed at a studio audience, which shouted back. High-pitched beeps obscured the obscenities. Amelia had no idea what any of it was about.

"The future," Calvin said. "Shoot."

"What's the plan? What are we going to tell them?" Amelia could hear her voice rising but had lost the power to control it. "What am I to you?"

"You're a little high-strung, you know that?" Calvin poked through the plastic grocery bags. They were down to a box of saltines and two bruised apples.

"When you look at me," Amelia said, "what do you see?"

"I'm getting sick of these questions." Calvin tossed an apple to Amelia. It hit her in the thigh. She clutched her leg, pretending the hit hurt more than it did. Calvin turned back to the TV.

"Is this who you really are?" Amelia asked. "A television junkie?"

"Welcome to SAS," Calvin said.

That evening when he said he was going to the store, he did not ask Amelia to come with him. She stared at her reflection in the turned-off television and thought about the grocery store clerk, Calvin pulling down her top, freeing her breasts, heavy and supple in his hands, the images so clear that Amelia knew them to be true. She had given up everything for this man, and at that very moment he was betraying her.

She decided to slit her wrists but could find nothing sharp enough in his bag or hers. She searched the room, her panic growing as she opened the dresser drawers, the nightstand, the closet. She even lifted the mattress. In the bathroom, she noticed the water tumblers. She slammed one against the counter; it broke with ease.

When he returned fifteen minutes later, he found her crouched naked in the bathtub, slicing at her wrists with a jagged shard of glass.

✳

"I COULDN'T GO DEEP enough," she told me. "I tried and tried, but my hands just wouldn't do it. Dying is a lot harder than you'd think."

The lines were pink, superficial. I thought of our playacting as children, Amelia in the starring role of dying Sara. I knew my part. I lifted her wrists to my lips and kissed her wounds.

She pulled her hands away.

"They're sore," she said.

"You have to tell Tammy. She thinks he raped you."

The Band-Aids dangled from Amelia's wrists. She tried to press them back into place.

"Maybe he did," she said.

"Did he?"

"Carrie, don't you get it? The truth doesn't matter. They'll believe what they want, and I don't care. I don't owe them an explanation. Not after everything they've done to us."

"What have they done?"

"This." She waved her hand in a circle. "It's a prison. It's bullshit. You want to know the truth? We're no better than anyone else."

She ripped the Band-Aids off, dropped them on the ground.

"I wish I'd never come back," she said.

"What about me? Did you think about what I'd do if you left? If you *died*?"

"At times like those," she said, "you don't."

I understood then what I had been trying so hard to deny: I had not bestowed freedom on Amelia with saintly self-sacrifice; she had abandoned me. She had turned her back without giving me a second thought. The wounds on her wrists lost their romance, and I saw a traitor sitting across from me.

"You're nothing like Sara," I said.

The swiftest, deepest cut I could deliver.

I left her there in the clearing, the sun beating down on her shameful scars.

seven

ONE MOMENT I WAS running through his cabin, calling his name, and the next I was at Home. I must have flown down the path; I have no memory of my feet ever touching the ground. I was on a noble mission and nothing would stop me, not even the memory of Amelia's face, her shock and hurt. I hadn't heard her call after me, but I decided that she must have and seen me not turn around, not even hesitate my step.

I found Robert in the kitchen, scrubbing pots. Nearby Meg chopped onions.

He did not look up, even after I'd stumbled to a halt beside him.

"We're working." He kept his voice low, but Meg's knife hesitated over the cutting board. "Can't this wait?"

"No," I said and walked out.

He did not speed up to meet me. When I slowed, he stayed behind.

At the pond he came up next to me. We stood shoulder to shoulder, looking into the muddy water.

"This is a sensitive time," he said. "I thought I'd been clear."

I reached for his fingers. He let me take them. Our hands hung between us, like father and daughter.

I told him Amelia's story as if it were my own.

When I finished, he said, "Where is she?"

I pointed to the woods.

He went running.

I began to follow, but he shouted, "No. Stay."

As if he were commanding a dog.

I obeyed.

✳

I WOULD HAVE WAITED there until the end of time, but Glory called to me. On our porch she stood with one hand shielding her eyes, the other holding an orange plastic bucket.

"I'm busy," I said.

"Doing what?"

Saving my life.

How could I answer in words she'd understand?

She slapped the bucket against her thigh. "Come on," she said. "There's work to be done."

eight

AN HOUR BEFORE DINNER the old church bell rang at Home, signaling an emergency meeting. The bell was used rarely, sounded once or twice a year to warn of tornado sightings, heavy snowfall predictions, but here we were in the middle of June, the sky clear with only the slightest hint of a breeze. I remember the exact texture of the air, its almost impossible smoothness, the childish scents of warm grass and soap. Since then I've experienced many such afternoons—commonplace, unnoticed by most—and invariably the serenity makes me shudder.

On our hands and knees, Glory and I scrubbed our porch. I hadn't told her about what had occurred earlier that day, Amelia's story or Robert's reaction. I considered the matter to be private, over. I believed that soon Robert and Amelia would come for me and the three of us would walk off together into the woods to make our amends. What had been broken would be fixed.

When the bell rang, Glory rocked back on her heels, pushed her hair off her forehead, soap bubbles sticking to her eyebrows.

"What do you suppose that's about?" she said.

I wrung out the sponge and placed it beside the bucket.

"I bet Amelia's talked. What do you know?"

"Nothing," I said.

"You wouldn't tell me if you did."

She spoke in the same matter-of-fact tone she had used to tell me Mike would be leaving. No bitterness. Just resignation and acceptance.

I looked down at my feet streaked with dirt and bubbles. The bell kept ringing.

Glory held out her hand and I took it, bearing her weight as she stood. She straightened her shirt. "Well," she said, "at least Tammy will know we've been putting in an honest day's work."

We were among the last to arrive at the meeting room. Someone had brought in chairs from the dining room and arranged them in a semicircle. In the center Tammy stood with head bowed and hands clasped.

Across the room Mike sat between Meg and Eddie. Meg wore a scooped neck t-shirt, the tops of her breasts visible, and a paisley skirt that fell to the floor. I'd known her all my life as one of the mother figures, moving efficiently in the background, but lately I'd started to notice her more, to view her differently—as a threat. I'd seen the way Robert followed her with his eyes; I'd watched her place her hand on the small of Mike's back in the kitchen; and I'd come to understand what I had witnessed as a child, Mike and Meg walking up the path in the middle of the night, his arm around her waist not to help her but to bring her body close. They'd been having sex for years.

I wanted to believe the same wasn't true for Robert. When I'd asked him, he'd laughed and insisted he had no interest in Meg beyond friendship. But that had been weeks ago, before Amelia ran away with Calvin, before Robert told me that that had to be it for a while.

Beside me Glory fidgeted, her ponytail drooping, her body invisible inside baggy jeans and a man's work shirt, the sleeves rolled up to reveal banged-up elbows. She belonged to a different species than Meg, one I was afraid I belonged to, too. I couldn't remember the last time my mother had looked beautiful, and I hated Meg for adding to the wrinkles around my mother's mouth, the premature gray in her hair.

I put my hand on Glory's shoulder and guided her to the two empty chairs by the door.

Tammy pressed her palms together, signaling the start of the meeting.

Where were Amelia and Robert?

"Namaste," Tammy said.

Around the semi-circle, the thirteen members of Orion repeated the greeting, so familiar to us that we had forgotten the meaning, if we had ever truly known it.

I watched the door; at any moment Amelia and Robert would walk in. They'd be in trouble for not adhering to the bell, but I would help them with the extra chores Tammy would assign. After all, it was my fault. I imagined them deep in the woods, deeper than I had ever gone with either of them. Under trees so dense no light came through, he had his arms around her, stroking her hair as she said she was so, so sorry.

Miraculously, the scars on her wrists vanished.

The silence drew out. The members of Orion shifted, folding chairs squeaking.

Tammy played with the perfume ball at her neck, lifting the pendant, dropping it, lifting it again.

"Today is a very sad day," she said.

The perfume ball dropped.

She looked at me.

"Robert and Amelia Holbrook—"

"They'll be here any second," I said. "I don't think they heard the bell."

"Robert and Amelia have left us."

From around the room, murmurs.

"No—just give them a minute."

"Carrie," Tammy said. "I know this will be especially hard for you, but you must listen. They've gone. They won't be returning."

"What happened?" Meg said.

Slowly Tammy turned toward Meg. "We came to an understanding," she said. "Their values and ours no longer coincided."

"That's not true," I said.

"No?" Tammy snapped back to me. "I have no reason to lie. After we're done here, you can go to their cabin and check for yourself."

I started to get up, but Glory grabbed my arm and pushed me back into the chair. She leaned across me, pinning me into place.

"Don't," she whispered. "Do not."

"Is this common?" Betty asked. She was just two weeks in, an older woman with a blond pageboy, roots beginning to show. Round-eyed, she looked around the room, as if taking us all in for the first time.

"No," Tammy said. "Not under these circumstances. Robert and Amelia had made their lives here. I thought they would be with us forever, but we have been shown that no one is immune to the temptations of SAS. I believed them to be different. Special. But I was wrong. We all must fight that much harder."

"So they just left?" Meg said. "Without saying goodbye?"

"We decide that would be for the best."

I tried to slip underneath Glory's arm, but she held me fast. Her hand clamped over my mouth.

"We must come together," Tammy said, "to cleanse this space. To cleanse our spirits so that we, too, may not be led off course."

She lowered herself onto the floor.

One by one, the members of Orion followed.

"Let us meditate on purity."

They closed their eyes, positioned their hands in prayer.

They joined voices.

OM.

Except for Glory.

She stayed right next to me and began to hiccup, her body jerking as if punched. When she moved her hand from my mouth to cover her own, I broke free.

✳

Their cabin door, open.

Inside: the table, the bench.

Their mugs, side by side on the windowsill.

The water bucket next to the stove.

The dented pillows on the beds. The blankets neatly folded.

The rubber bands Amelia wore in her hair. The long, iridescent feather we'd found in our spot behind the pond and decided must have come from a griffin. The three apple-head dolls Tammy had made, one of which had lost its head years before.

A block of wood on the table. Robert's penknife.

Tammy had lied. She was punishing Amelia for Calvin, punishing Robert for Amelia, punishing me for loving them both.

They would return, and when they did, they would find me waiting.

I turned toward the door.

The shelf for Sara's shrine—empty.

✳

I CRAWLED AMONG THE pond grasses. I wanted to throw up, but leaning over the clouded water, nothing came.

Fingertips formed slow, concentric circles across my back.

"Sweetheart," Glory said. "Hush. Everything will be all right."

Sweetheart.

She hadn't called me sweetheart since I was a little girl.

"Go away."

The motion stopped, but her fingers stayed, pressing against my neck.

"Please," I said.

When night fell, I lay down in the mud. I thought about slipping under the water, opening my mouth, letting the sludge fill my body, letting the mud suck me in.

How could they have left without me?

I screamed and the night answered back. The sound broke apart into sobs that left my body hollowed out, every bone scraped clean.

I listened to the crickets.

The water rippling.

The hoot of an owl.

✳

I WOKE IN MY bed, my arms and legs covered in mosquito bites.

Glory stood in the doorway, watching as I scratched myself bloody.

"Good morning, sweetheart," she said.

She sat down on the bed. When I rolled away, she grabbed my shoulders and made me look her in the face.

"Tammy loved them," she said. "She loves you."

"Stop lying," I said.

Glory stood and smoothed the skirt of her dress, her nicest one.

"Tammy's a good woman," she said. "She didn't have to make this place. She didn't have to give us a home."

"We didn't have to come."

Glory was quiet. I tried not to look at her, but I couldn't help it. She was crying.

"I wanted to give you a good life," she said.

"You mean give yourself one."

"All right," she said. "Yes. What's so wrong about that?"

"Has it been good? Are you happy?"

She yanked off the blanket, threw it on the floor.

"It isn't Tammy's fault," she said. "You know that. There's something about Robert and Amelia that you aren't telling. You're pretending that you don't know, but you do."

I curled onto my side, brought my knees to my chest.

"Fine," she said. "Keep your secrets."

She threw the blanket over me. The world went dark. I took deep breaths of wool; the scent soothed me.

I needed to think. I needed to come up with a plan.

Her hand on my arm jolted me; I thought she'd left.

"Get dressed," Glory said, "and go to breakfast. Stop making this hard for the rest of us."

For you. I mouthed the words, fuzzies from the blanket sticking to my tongue. For you. For you. For you.

I wrapped the blanket tighter around me. After a while I heard the floorboards creak. I poked my head out and saw Glory moving outside the window, heading up the path.

The door to their cabin still stood open.

nine

No one came to get me. I imagined the excuses Glory made: she needs her sleep, she had a late night, she just needs to cry it out. She was so attached to them, you know. Carrie and Amelia—like sisters. We can't expect her to just bounce back.

From the garden I could hear their voices. The scrape of silverware. Meg's braying laughter.

I began with the tomatoes. I ripped off the fruit and squeezed, juice running over my fingers and toes.

I broke the cornstalks in two.

I flung the carrots as far as I could.

I raised my knees high and stomped through the lettuce.

I kicked up the strawberries.

I got down on all fours and rooted through the dirt, digging everything up, turning everything over.

Burrowing.

Until the earth covered me over. Until I disappeared.

✳

SHOUTING.

Tammy running.

She grabbed me by the neck, lifted me off the ground.

"What have you done?"

She slapped me. Tammy, who did not believe in violence, who'd punished us for shooting at trees with a bow and arrow. My hand went to where hers had been. My cheek throbbed, but the warmth comforted me, let me know I'd done what I'd set out to do.

"Liar," I shouted. "Hypocrite."

Her mouth hung open. She started toward me again, but Mike pulled her back. The rest swarmed around Tammy, rubbing her shoulders, looping arms around her waist. Only Glory stood apart. As they went inside, she came to me.

"Why?" she said. "What was the point?"

She stooped and brushed dirt off my legs with slaps that stung almost as much as Tammy's.

"Do you want to get us kicked out, too?" she said.

When I didn't answer, she took me by the hand and, without looking at me, led me into Home.

✳

THEY SAT ME IN the meeting room, Eddie stationed at the door to prevent me from escaping. I stared at the low shelves crammed with books that Amelia and I had long outgrown, our child-sized chairs stacked on top of each other in the corner. I tried to picture Robert and Amelia at Mosey Inn, Room Five, sleeping late beneath the picture of kittens in a wicker basket. But if that were the case, they already would have come back for me. In the middle of the night, they would have snuck in, plucked me from my bed.

Instead I pictured them on a bus, on the way to Chicago. I didn't know how long the trip took; they could be there now, sitting at Sara's kitchen table, eating breakfast.

How would I ever find them in Chicago?

After what felt like hours, Tammy entered, followed by Glory and Mike.

"Why did you destroy the garden?" she said.

Glory wiped her eyes; Mike wouldn't look at me.

"I hated it," I said. "I hate you."

"Your anger is misdirected."

"They didn't have to go."

Tammy squatted, planting her hands on my knees.

"They did," she said. "I'd known for a while that a change had occurred, and I should have taken action sooner. Their negative energy was radiating outward, infecting all of us." She squeezed my knees. "Especially you."

I shifted, trying to dislodge her hands, but she pressed down, her forearms locking my legs together.

"The destruction of the garden is proof enough of that," she said.

"That's not their fault. They're not even here."

"Maybe so, but I have talked to Glory and Mike. They have witnessed changes in you this past year. Secretiveness. Argumentativeness. Laziness."

I looked at my parents standing behind Tammy.

"Who are you to talk?" I said to them.

Glory pinched the skin at the base of her throat, her mouth opening and closing, opening and closing. Mike turned around so he faced the back of the room.

"Concerns have come to light," Tammy said, "about your relationship with Robert."

"My relationship?"

"You were too close."

"Compared to what?"

"Compared to the way a child should be with a man."

"At least Robert loved me." I threw my arm toward Mike. "He won't even look at me."

"Did he tell you that?" Tammy said. "Did he say he loved you?"

I met her eyes, green and unblinking, like the eyes of a cat.

"We told each other."

"The relationship. Was it intimate?"

"We're all equal. That's what you told us. The children and the adults."

Tammy stood. "You're twisting my words."

"No, that's exactly what you said. We're all equal and we all have free will."

"You've been misled. He used those words against me. Against the good of this community."

"He's not saying them. I am."

"We didn't know," Glory said in a rush. "Not the full extent. If we had known, we would have stopped it. We never would have let—"

"Shut up," Mike said.

Glory started crying again. Tammy stared at her.

"I don't like any of this," Tammy said.

"If you want us to go," Mike said, "we'll go."

"The garden." Tammy looked down at me. "Considering what happened to you, I am willing to forgive, if you promise to atone."

"I won't," I said.

"I see."

"I'd do it again and again and again."

"Then you're giving me no choice."

"That's it?" Glory said. "You'll send us away, just like that?"

"Why shouldn't I? Rules have been broken. The atmosphere has been corrupted beyond any redeemable point. I have a community to take care of, and the needs of the collective supersede the wants of the individual. You should know that. After all of these years. I'd thought that you—I'd trusted that you—the five of you—"

Tammy stopped talking. She folded her hands, took a deep breath.

"Enough," she said.

✳

WE HAD TWO HOURS.

Glory shut herself in the bedroom. From the porch, Mike and I listened to her sobs. He still wouldn't look at me.

"I've got stuff to take care of," he said and jumped down the steps.

A few minutes later Glory came onto the porch. She'd stopped crying; she'd even brushed her hair.

"Where's your father?"

I pointed toward the path.

She lifted her hair, fanned the back of her neck.

"Hot," she said, "isn't it?"

I couldn't stop shivering.

"I'm sorry," I said.

"About the garden? Or Robert? Or which of a million things?"

I couldn't answer.

"Well," she said, "I am, too, but we hardly have time for that now."

She went back into the cabin and returned with a set of keys, which she dropped on the step beside me.

"Time to get cracking," she said.

ten

THE BACK DOORS OF the station wagon had rusted shut. We pulled, the two of us together, with all our strength to open them. I was surprised the car ran. It had been parked behind the cabin, gradually eclipsed by weeds, for years.

We owned so little now: just three backpacks stuffed with clothes. We left behind the kitchenware, my schoolbooks, our sheets and blankets. Those weren't ours. Technically, nothing was. We were stealing, which, as Amelia had said on my first day at Orion, was especially bad here.

Mike returned with his hands jammed in his pockets, his shoulders around his ears, kicking at stones along the path like a belligerent teenager.

"How's Meg?" Glory asked.

"I wouldn't know. I went to see Tammy."

"What for?"

"The deposit. I've got half. She'll mail the rest later."

"Mail it where?"

"Wherever we end up."

I felt my parents' shame draped across me, weighing me down as I lay on the backseat and closed my eyes. The car rocked and swayed down the path. I didn't look to see if anyone had come to see us off, but later Glory said that Meg and Betty had been there. They didn't wave. They just stood outside Home with their arms linked and watched the car pass.

We circled through the Cuyahoga Valley like fledgling birds, unsure of what our wings could do. As the sun set Glory mentioned Cleveland, her parents.

"But not tonight," she said. "I can't handle them tonight." She turned in the seat, her body arched awkwardly, to look at me. "Hungry, sweetheart?"

I wished she would stop calling me that. Sweetheart wasn't her; it wasn't me.

I shook my head.

"No one's hungry," Mike said.

"Come on, it'll give us something to do. Let us think for a moment."

At the next exit he pulled off the highway and into the parking lot of Aunt Sal's Family Restaurant. The place was packed. We were seated at a booth next to the restrooms, behind a family of four with a toddler who kept standing up on the seat and staring at us over the fake walnut divide. Glory waved at him, and he blew out his cheeks, stuck out his tongue.

"Cute," Glory said.

Mike sighed and wiped at the table with a napkin.

The waitresses wore gingham dresses and calico bonnets. The fabrics clashed, as if chosen randomly from a pile. Our teenage waitress chewed her lip as she tapped her pen against her notepad.

"We'll have three salads, no cheese, no dressing," Glory said.

"No, two salads," Mike said. "I'll have the cheeseburger."

"Seriously?"

"I've never been more serious."

"You're going to get sick," Glory said.

Mike passed the menus to the waitress and looked across the table at me.

"What do you have to say for yourself?" he said.

At the booth behind us, the mother yelled at her son, "Once more, and Mr. Binkie goes bye-bye." The child howled.

"What a charade," Mike said. "The utopian dream? How many times has that been tried and failed?"

"Maybe you should have asked those questions earlier," Glory said, straightening the salt and pepper shakers.

"I did. You didn't want to hear me."

"I'm not taking all the blame."

"Hey, he fooled me, too. I admit it. I thought he was a good guy. An upstanding guy. Whatever the hell that means."

"He is a good guy," I said.

My parents flinched as if they'd forgotten I was there.

"He's not what you think," I said. "It wasn't like that."

But I couldn't explain. Not to my parents, sitting across the table in this cheesy, perfectly SAS restaurant on our first night in nine years as part of the outside world. My mother cocked her head. My father frowned, his brow heavy. Robert and Amelia were gone. I had no way to contact them, no way of finding out where they went. I wanted to curl into the corner of the booth and never move.

"Did you have sex with him?" Glory said, but I could only shake my head.

"We'll get you counseling," she said.

But they never did. After that night we never spoke of my relationship with Robert again.

The food arrived, and we ate ravenously, thankful for something to do. Grease dripped from Mike's cheeseburger. Out in the parking lot, he did get sick, vomiting into the bushes while Glory and I leaned against the trunk of the car and watched the lights come on along the highway.

We stayed at a motel like Mosey Inn. There was only one bed, a queen, and we all slept together, Mike on one side of Glory, me on the other, the way we had slept long ago when I was very young and plagued by nightmares of monsters in the closet, dragons outside the window, goblins under the bed. Just like then, I couldn't sleep. Beside me I sensed Glory's taut wakefulness, even though she made no sound. Mike snored. As the night wore on, his reverberations became louder until they seemed to shake the room.

✳

He left us four days later. Glory and I came back from grocery shopping to find the note on the dresser, along with a neat pile of twenty-dollar bills. She read the note, tore it apart, flushed the pieces down the toilet. She walked out, leaving the door open. I understood not to follow. I sat on the bed and counted the money: fifteen hundred dollars. A warm breeze came through the room, blowing the bathroom door shut. An hour passed. I decided to wait another hour before I began to worry.

Twenty minutes later, Glory returned. The skin around her eyes looked raw, but she was no longer crying. She lay down on her stomach on the floor.

"Sweetheart," she said. "Walk on my back."

"Why?"

"It hurts. Please, just do it."

I stepped gingerly onto her back. Beneath my toes, I felt the bones of her spine and ribs. If I jumped, I could break every last one. I could cripple her, or worse. The thought made me tender, and I took a tiny step up her spine, careful how I laid my weight.

She patted my ankle.

"I used to do this for your father," she said. "Now I see why he liked it."

In the morning she called her parents in Cleveland, taking the phone into the bathroom and shutting the door as far as it would go around the cord. I could still hear every word. Her need repulsed me. Within her sniffles and sobs and pleas for forgiveness, I heard a version of myself.

My throat tickled. I coughed, opened my mouth, moved my lips, but no sound came. I flung myself across the bed, my head hanging off the side. Once, in English lessons, Tammy had assigned us a story about a little boy who stopped speaking after his parents' death. She had explained that he made the choice to remain silent as a way to gain control over his trauma. Now I wondered if he had truly become physically incapable of speech. Maybe when your heart broke, you lost your ability to talk.

The bathroom door opened, and Glory emerged, upside down. "The prodigal daughters," she said, smiling. "Aren't we a pair?"

"What did they say?"

My fingers went to my throat, poking at the ridges. Against my will, my voice had returned.

"They said to come home," she said. "Can you believe it?"

I couldn't.

"But we'll only stay a little while," she said.

The next day we drove to the city. My grandparents were strangers; try as I might, I could find no traces of someone I used to know. Their skin clung loosely to their bones. Their eyes bulged in their heads. They could not remember my name. "Christie," my grandmother called me. "Clara," my grandfather corrected her.

My grandmother made meatloaf for dinner. Across the table Glory looked at me and nodded. I watched her take a bite, swallow, and take another before taking one myself. The texture disgusted me more than the taste; I felt like I was eating part of me. After each bite I took a long drink of water, and somehow, I made it through the meal. In bed my stomach cramped. I lay in agony, unable to call for help. Glory appeared with a damp washcloth and wiped my face.

"It'll get better," she said. "I promise."

By the end of the first week she'd found a job. Within three months she'd moved us out to the suburbs.

✳

And so, at the age of fourteen, my life started over.

We were supposed to forget everything.

"My good girl," Glory said as I sat at the kitchen table and did my homework. I was behind in every subject, but with the help of tutors, I entered ninth grade in the fall.

"My good, good girl," she'd say, pulling my hair off my neck, and I couldn't help it, I thought about the way Robert had kissed the knob of my spine, his sturdy hands on my shoulders, rooting me down.

eleven

THE POSTCARDS BEGAN ARRIVING the spring after I turned sixteen. I'd find them in the mailbox after school, slipped innocently between ads for Dillard's and the Visa bill. They were spaced far enough apart that I never really believed one would be there, yet whenever I approached the mailbox, I felt dizzy with hope. Once I had the card in my hand, relief would come over me like a fever, and I would race upstairs to my room and shut the door even though I had the house to myself. I'd sit on the bed and stare at the picture, trying to divine at least this one's meaning, until Glory came home from work.

The images were from all over Ohio, Kentucky, and Pennsylvania. The first: a red brick building at Hale Farm and Village, a history museum not far from Orion. The next: polar bears at the Cleveland Zoo. A horse park outside of Lexington. The Ohio River at sunset. An Amish buggy on a lonely road. Some were nonsensical: a woman in Victorian dress playing a piano, a flowerpot on her head; a teddy bear hugging a real rabbit smoking a cigar; a man with a long mustache dressed as a Roman solider and brandishing a sword.

No images of Chicago. She had not gone without me.

A month passed between the first postcard and the second. Six weeks between the second and third. Then they began coming more frequently. Once a week, twice a week. By fall, they were arriving every other day.

The backs contained no messages, only my address written in a hand as familiar to me as my own.

All of the postmarks were from towns in Ohio. I wrote the

names down and during study hall went to the library and looked them up in the atlas. All were within a fifty-mile radius of where I lived, but she didn't use any one consistently or more often than another. I'd hoped she was zeroing in, about to make a flesh-and-blood arrival, but the most recent postcard had been sent from the town farthest away.

At first I taped the postcards in chronological order above my bed. Then I took them down and arranged them by place. But that didn't make sense either. I grouped them by type of image: natural, historical, humorous. I even tried putting them together by most prominent color, gradating from light to dark. I stood back and squinted at the wall above my bed as if the cards were a Magic Eye, but I only made my head hurt.

Every time a new card arrived, I would send up a prayer to Amelia, wherever she might be, asking her to please, please tell me what she wanted.

✳

Shortly before my seventeenth birthday, the postcards stopped. I felt their absence like a severed limb, certain I saw a corner peeking out from underneath the electric bill or among the pages of Glory's *Good Housekeeping.* I dreamt of glossy photographs of the Columbus skyline, sailboats on Lake Erie, fields of golden corn, and woke with my fingers clenched. I turned on the light and recounted the postcards above my bed. Always, the number remained the same.

✳

In the middle of January, the phone calls began.

Glory answered the first. Doing homework on the sofa, I

heard her in the kitchen, her voice starting strong and confident but growing weaker with each successive "hello." After she hung up, she came to the doorway and stood with folded arms.

"That was odd," she said.

I turned the pages of my history book, past maps of Civil War battlefields and pencil sketches of Union soldiers. "A wrong number," I said.

"They didn't say anything. Just breathing."

"A creep."

She pinched her throat. "What's that you dial to get the last number that called? Star something?"

"Why would you want to call them back?"

"If it happens again," she said, "I will."

It did happen again, the next night, and the next.

The next day she called just after four o'clock in the afternoon, when I would be home from school and Glory still at work.

Even her silence was recognizable. For a full minute I just listened.

"Amelia," I said. "I know it's you. Where are you?"

"You bitch."

Her words, an electrical shock coursing down the phone line, searing my fingers; I almost dropped the phone.

"Don't hang up," I said.

But the dial tone beeped in my ear.

I sat at the kitchen table and waited. I knew she would call back. The insult had been perfunctory, a ritual we had to get through, a way of keeping me on my toes. She'd sought me out, which meant she needed me as much as I needed her.

Five minutes later, the phone rang again.

"I want to see you," she said. "Will you meet me?"

✳

For the previous year Amelia had been living with her aunt less than ten miles away; we'd shared the same grocery store, the same mall, the same movie theater. Our high school sports teams were each other's chief rivals. The proximity seemed like a trick, meant to teach me some sort of lesson, like when she'd demanded my necklace on my first day at Orion. And just like then the way her laughter was edged with meanness made me want to be with her, to be her, even more.

She understood the world so much better than I ever could.

We met on Saturday at the McDonald's in the sprawling commercial district between my town and hers. She drove the used car her aunt had given her for her birthday. I hadn't learned to drive yet, so I walked.

She was already there, seated in the window. She'd ordered us both coffees. She looked skinny, but her hair hung to her shoulders in fashionable layers and she wore makeup applied with a precision neither Glory nor I could accomplish, despite our sporadic best efforts.

We smiled shyly at each other.

"How are you?" she said.

"Okay," I said. "You?"

"All right." She sipped her coffee. "Thank you."

I wanted to lean across the table and kiss her.

The coffee tasted terrible. We drank it anyway. Over the rims of our cups, we cast each other embarrassed glances. I began to fear that our reunion would be one long, uncomfortable silence.

I should have known better. Amelia had stories to tell. She didn't speak of Orion or Robert or what had happened between us; she talked about her English class and her teacher, Mr. Aronson, who was encouraging her to write poetry. She talked about her new friends. She seemed to have a lot of them, but she spoke in a mocking tone, satirizing their trips to the mall, belittling the homecoming dance, although she had gone, wearing a strapless, periwinkle gown with a rhinestone bodice, the star soccer player, Kevin, as her date. She talked about her aunt's house. "The epitome of SAS," she said, her eyes shining with delight. "She put a TV in my room. And a VCR. Everyone's jealous. They come over and watch stupid movies for hours, cooing over the 'hot' boys. They think about nothing but clothes and makeup and when they're finally going to get laid."

I rolled my eyes, but I desperately wanted to be one of those girls heaped on Amelia's bed, sharing a big bowl of popcorn, painting each other's nails.

Amelia's self-possession was magical. She could walk through walls.

"Now you tell me," she said.

I took a long drink of coffee, sinking my teeth into the waxy rim of the cup. "I go to school," I said. "I come home."

She looked out at the parking lot. Sleet had begun to fall. A blue Buick pulled slowly out of the parking space in front of the window, and I had the realization, as sudden and clear as an epiphany, that everything out here moved slowly, lumbering stupidly through life. That, in fact, was the whole problem.

"We have free will," Amelia said. "Remember the importance of personal choice and individual impact?"

She rolled up the sleeve of her sweater and twisted so that the back of her arm faced me. There, in the skin above the elbow, were long, pink scratch marks.

"See?" she said. "Free will."

"You did that?"

I touched the longest scratch with my thumb, following it up until it disappeared beneath Amelia's sleeve. They reminded me of the scars on her wrists, her half-hearted suicide attempt.

When I looked up, she was grinning.

"You shouldn't hurt yourself," I said.

She pushed her sleeve down and leaned forward, lowering her voice. "I'm going to get out of here soon. I'm going to New York."

"Chicago," I said.

"New York. Where I can be no one."

"You'll always be someone."

Her face colored, the first time I could remember seeing her blush.

"That's a corny line, Carrie."

"What will you do in New York?"

"Find a place to stay. Sleep on park benches if I have to. Write. This poetry thing, it's for real. I think it's my true voice."

"Can I read your poems?"

"Maybe later."

"Where's Robert?"

"I was wondering when you were going to ask that," she said, but she didn't answer.

In my coat pocket was the letter I'd written Robert the night before. I'd demanded an explanation for why he'd left me, why he'd taken Amelia away, when he had promised to always protect me and keep me with them. I wrote that I hated him and crossed it out because that wasn't true: I only hated him some of the time; the rest of the time I missed him. Instead I wrote that I was angry. Life since Orion had been horrible: scary at first and now just nothing. Numb. I wanted to feel alive again. I wanted to feel like I mattered, like I was loved. I asked if anything he'd ever told me had been true. I asked if Sara was really alive.

But now did not seem like the right time to give Amelia the letter.

She downed the rest of her coffee. I followed suit, even though the coffee had gone cold. She slammed her empty cup on the table.

"Let's go for a drive," she said.

I didn't know where Amelia was taking me, and I didn't care.

"You're too trusting," she said. "That's always been your problem. When we were kids, you did whatever I told you."

"I could trust you," I said.

"You still think so?"

Amelia pulled into a new sub-development, down winding roads, past lots dimly lit by driveway lights, the shadowed houses large and cumbersome in the style of the moment. We reached a dead end, and Amelia parked.

"There," she said, pointing to a Tudor down the street. "That's where I live."

"Nice," I said.

Amelia snorted.

But I meant it. The house looked nice, with neatly trimmed hedges and a covered backyard pool. A light shone in an upstairs window, and I thought about Glory, who must have been back by now from the Cleveland home and garden show she'd gone to with friends from work. She would wonder where I was, but she had no one to call to ask my whereabouts. She would make herself a cup of tea, sit down on the sofa with one of her decorating magazines, and wait. I should have felt guilty, but I didn't. I was caught inside a dream.

"Aunt Louise," Amelia said. "She wants me to call her Lou, but I won't. I didn't even know she existed until Robert dropped me on her doorstep."

I squinted at the house, half-expecting Aunt Louise to materialize right there, in the side yard. I imagined that she looked like an older version of Amelia, and I wanted to see her, to get a glimpse of what the future held. Somehow I expected that I would understand myself better then, too.

"Want to know why he did it?" she said. "I asked about Sara. The liar swore up and down she'd died. Bled to death. He passed out right after that. He'd been on a drinking binge for days. The next morning he brought me here. Said go meet your aunt. Drove away without even waving. The weirdest thing was she had my room all set up. Like they'd planned it all along."

"Robert doesn't drink."

Amelia looked at me. "He hasn't had a sober day since we left Orion."

A cold knot formed in my stomach.

"He wasn't who you thought he was," she said. "You know that right?"

I nodded.

"None of them were. They were all fucking. Every coupling you could imagine. All that bullshit Tammy spouted about purity. They lied to us through their teeth."

"I know Mike and Meg had a thing, but—"

"Ask Glory."

Amelia started the car.

"I'm sorry," I said. "I didn't think Tammy would find out. I didn't think she'd make you leave."

"Yeah, well." Amelia swung the car around. "We all learned something that day."

"I'm sorry about that, too," I said.

She kept her eyes on the road.

"Are you going to look for Sara?"

"What's the point?" she said. "The last thing I need is another adult in my life."

"You can't just forget her."

"Right now, my main priority is myself. And yours should be, too. We don't owe anybody anything."

We drove in silence, but after a few minutes, the quiet lost its tension and became companionable again. In the driver's seat of a passing pickup, I saw a boy from my math class. He was wearing a Cleveland Browns snowcap and drumming his hands on the steering wheel. When he saw me, he raised three fingers in salute. I nodded back. Our exchange struck me as unbelievable—how could he see me here, when I had separated so completely from his world?

"Look," I said to Amelia, but he was already behind us. She didn't seem to hear me anyway.

As I had expected, the living room light was on. "Just drop me here," I said, but Amelia pulled into the driveway.

The front door did not open. No worried shape appeared in the living room window.

"When are you going to New York?" I said.

"Summer. Maybe spring."

"I'll come with you."

"Right."

"Really. It's better that way. Traveling alone isn't any fun. You need someone to depend on. To help out."

"You have plans," Amelia said. "You have college."

"Don't you want to go to college?"

She reached across me and popped open the passenger door.

"This was nice," she said. "We'll do it again."

"Promise?"

When she didn't answer, I took the letter from my pocket and stuffed it in her hand.

Amelia looked at the envelope. The corners were bent. I should have been more careful.

"Carrie," she said, trying to hand the letter back.

"You can read it if you want."

She put the letter in her purse and grabbed my shoulders, pulling me against her. She held on for only a second before pushing me away.

"Take care of yourself," she said.

I stepped out of the car. As she backed out of the driveway, I made a point of remembering how she looked—her neck twisted to see the road, her hair falling into her face as she turned the wheel—because I knew I would never see her again.

I found Glory on the sofa, just as I had pictured her. She put her finger in her magazine to mark her place.

"I was with Amelia," I said.

"Your jeans are dirty. Go get changed and we'll have dinner."

"Did you hear me? I was with Amelia."

Glory reopened her magazine. "I thought that's where you were. Are you going to see her again?"

I looked at the page she was reading. *Four ways to bind a scrapbook.*

"Scrapbooking?" I said. "You don't have any pictures to put in one."

"Are you going to see her again?"

"Probably not."

"There's a spinach soufflé in the oven. It'll be done in ten minutes."

"Did you sleep with other people at Orion?"

She looked up. "What?"

"Amelia said all the adults were sleeping with each other."

"That girl has always liked to tell stories."

"So it's not true?"

"I was faithful to your father."

Her answer relieved me. I went upstairs and changed into my pajamas. When I came back down, Glory had the table set and poured a glass of milk for me. While we ate, she talked about her day, her friend's plans for a new patio, her own burning desire for a different wallpaper pattern for the half-bath. She spooned a second helping of soufflé onto my plate and followed it up with chocolate cake and vanilla ice cream for dessert. For every gesture she made, every question she didn't ask, I was grateful. Her efforts at normalcy were a balm soothing a hurt I didn't want to admit but felt, stinging, all the same.

✳

AT THE END OF my senior year of high school, a postcard arrived. By then I had taken the others down from the wall above my bed, moving them first to my desk drawer and then, during a fit of spring cleaning inspired by my acceptance into college ("New beginnings," Glory said, "deserve a clean start."), into the wastebasket.

Black and white, this postcard showed the Brooklyn Bridge at night, the Manhattan skyline shimmering beyond. She included no message, but she didn't need to.

I carried the postcard from the mailbox to the house, where I tore it in two and threw the halves away in the trash below the kitchen sink.

Two years would pass before the next postcard, which arrived in my mailbox at the student union. In this one, the Brooklyn Bridge rises out of a dense fog, and I thought of the pond between our cabins, the haze that would form on hot summer mornings. Done with being angry, done with trying to move on, I pinned the postcard to my bulletin board and daydreamed about quitting school, going to New York, tracking Amelia down. But I never opened a New York City phonebook. I never called information. That didn't mean I wanted her to stop. She was creating the story, and as always, I wanted to know the ending. I just needed to remember my part, and every time I started to forget, she would send another postcard to remind me.

January

one

AMELIA KNOCKS ON MY front door.

I put down the magazine I've been reading, one of Glory's decorating castoffs. The clock on the bookshelf reads nine-twenty, which means I have been sitting here for three hours. I've forgotten to eat again.

I look down at the magazine, open to a recipe for devil's food cake. A grinning woman holds a perfect cake out on a silver platter, everything about her grotesque, from her wide-open blue eyes to the bell sleeves of her red blouse.

Please, I think, and Amelia knocks again.

Flesh and blood, there she is, spotlighted on my porch.

"Happy birthday," she says and gives me a bashful smile, as if she is showing up more than a week late for my party.

She wears a blue wool coat and matching beret, her hair tucked behind her ears. She seems taller, and when I look down, I see that she is wearing knee-high boots with pointy toes and four-inch heels that would crush my feet and make me stumble. I have on sweatpants, one of Peter's old t-shirts.

"Amelia," I say.

She hugs me. For a moment, I don't know how to respond; it's as if I have never been hugged before. Slowly, my arms go around her. Through her coat, I feel the outline of her shoulder blades, the knob at the top of her spine. She is wearing perfume, an expensive brand I've squirted on my wrists at Macy's: orange blossoms, moss, a hint of lime.

We hold each other for a long time. I'm not sure which of us steps back first. Simultaneously, our arms fall to our sides.

"You got the postcard?" she says.

Her voice has grown huskier, as if she has a cold or has taken up smoking.

"Yes," I say.

I stand there stupidly. I want to touch her again, to make sure she is real. I want to lock the door, run upstairs, and hide underneath my bed.

She cranes her neck, looking around me into the house. Embarrassed, I step aside, and she slips past me, hesitates in the hall, her beret in her hands, before going into the living room.

In the center of the room she stands, unbuttoning her coat.

"You have a nice house," she says, and I cringe.

She makes her way around the room, stopping briefly in front of the television, the window, the bookshelves, studying the details of my life as if they are not very interesting exhibits in a museum. When she spots her poetry, she laughs.

"You like my poems?" she says.

"Some of them."

"And the others?"

"Some are hard to understand."

"Obscurity. That's the promise and problem of poetry. Or so I've been told." She picks up a photograph of Maya. "Your daughter?"

The photograph was taken two summers ago on our vacation to Prince Edward Island. Maya, small and satisfied, stands on top of a sand dune, the wind blowing her hair, her feet planted wide apart, her hands on her hips. That stance, I realize now, is Amelia's. Unknowingly, I must have inherited it, too.

"Maya," I say.

"She's beautiful."

"Thank you."

"I'm sorry," Amelia says, putting the photograph back on the shelf. "I should have known you have a daughter."

"How could you have known?"

"Research," she says. "Telepathy."

"If you'd given me an address," I say, and am angry. What game has she been playing for twenty-five years? What right does she have to show up at my house, expecting me to be waiting, willing?

Why am I waiting? Why am I willing?

"I sent you an address this time," she says.

She catches my eye and holds it.

"Do you have any tea?" she says.

"Tea?"

"It's cold out there. Feel." She presses her hands to my cheeks; they're ice.

The kitchen, with its sink full of dirty dishes, looks guilty, caught in the overhead light. As I put the kettle on the stove, I listen for sounds of Amelia but hear nothing. I glance into the living room: she is sitting on the sofa with her legs crossed, her purse on the coffee table. She picks up the decorating magazine, flips through, puts it down. The kettle whistles.

She comes into the kitchen. "Cups?"

I point to the cupboard to the right of the sink. She takes down two holiday mugs, an old fashioned Santa in a sleigh full of presents, another gift from Glory. I place a teabag in each mug, and Amelia fills the mugs with water. She nudges her shoulder against mine.

"Working together," she says. "Just like old times."

In the corner of the sofa, she tucks her legs beneath her. The blue of the coat brings out the blue of her eyes, and she looks perfect, like a model from the magazine.

"What else don't I know about you?" she says.

"I'm getting divorced."

"Men." She swivels her wrist, discounting Peter with a wave of her fingers. "They come and go. I'd like to meet Maya."

"She's in California. With her father."

"He has custody?"

"No. For the holidays."

The tea is too hot; I feel a blister forming on the tip of my tongue. I put the mug down and try to imagine what Maya is doing right now. It's dinnertime in California, but I don't know what Peter's kitchen looks like, what sort of food he cooks, whether he takes her out to eat. Not for fast food. He is a healthy eater, a concerned father. I try to picture them walking hand-in-hand along the beach, sand clinging to their toes, seagulls careening overhead, but I've never been to California. I have no point of reference.

Amelia reaches for her purse. "Is it all right if I smoke?"

"Not in the house."

"Why not?"

The question catches me off-guard. "I don't want my daughter inhaling the smoke."

"But she's not here," Amelia says and shakes her head sharply, as if reprimanding herself. "Sorry. That was rude. I'm trying to be more tactful. The older you get, the less charming a lack of tact becomes."

Her fingers play with the hem of her coat.

"I can hang that up," I say.

"I prefer to keep it on."

But a moment later she shrugs off her coat and lays it across her lap. She is wearing a white blouse, almost see-through; I can make out her jutting collarbones.

"How's Glory?" Amelia says.

"She's good."

"Is she the same?"

I think about Glory's condo situated on a street of identical buildings, all gray and blue siding and big panes of glass. At the end of her street is a pond, a fountain in the center. "I don't have to do a thing," Glory likes to brag. "When the grass needs cut the boys come and cut it. When the sidewalks need cleared, they clear them. It's pretty close to heaven on earth."

"She's everything she never wanted to be," I say.

"Aren't we all?"

"She's happy," I add, feeling misunderstood.

Amelia runs a hand through her hair. Static electricity makes strands stick up, creating a blond halo. "Good for Glory," she says.

"Robert called her. He told her you were missing."

Her forehead crinkles, but I know her features well—she is only faking confusion. "Did he?"

"The police went to your apartment."

"And? Did they find me?" She laughs. "Maybe I am missing. What does missing mean?"

"It means not being where you're supposed to be."

"In that case, I've been missing for years."

Just like her poems, she is leading me in circles.

She takes a metal cigarette case from her purse; it looks like the one Calvin used to have. The cigarettes, too, are hand-rolled.

"I'm not going to smoke," she says. "Just feeling one is almost enough."

"Why did you leave New York?"

"Aren't you glad to see me?"

"Of course I am."

"And the postcard? Were you glad to see it?"

"I wasn't sure what to make of it."

She plays with her cigarette, slipping it over and under her fingers. "I would have thought you'd be able to figure that out," she says.

"You want us to look for Sara."

"Bingo." She points the cigarette at me. "You in?"

"How do you know she's there?"

"I don't know. I've looked her up online, and there's nothing. No record of any kind. It's like she never existed."

"Maybe she didn't. Maybe we made her up."

"This isn't something to joke about, Carrie."

But I'm not joking.

I remember Amelia, my Sleeping Beauty, lying in the grass. When I lowered my ear to her chest, I heard no heartbeat. My tears came from a place so deep I've seldom accessed it since. We'd been perfect in our roles, powerful; we could have made the unreal real. We could have conjured anything.

Amelia leans across the sofa and takes my hand, her fingers still ice. They curl around mine, but I can't make my fingers do the same.

My hand just lies there, flat.

"I feel in my soul that my mother is in Chicago," Amelia says. "And I want us to find her together, just like we planned all those years ago."

"Why now?"

"Why not now? We're not getting younger, and neither is she. I'd like to find her before she dies. Again."

"And if we find her? Then what?"

Amelia reaches into her purse and removes a gold-plated lighter. She puts the cigarette between her lips, flicks the flame.

"Don't," I say, and her eyes pop.

"Shit," she says, dropping the lighter and unlit cigarette onto the table. "Sorry. I forgot."

Her transgression makes me feel braver. We are inside my house, where my rules apply.

"Robert told Glory you wrote him a suicide note," I say.

"Is that what he called it?"

"That's what she said."

"Well. I suppose that's a fairly accurate description."

"You're thinking of killing yourself?"

"No," Amelia says, rearranging her coat to cover her lap. "Not at this moment."

"You shouldn't."

"You don't really know," she says. "Do you?"

"Where is Robert?"

She stops fidgeting. Her eyes grow smaller, meaner, like I remember Sara's eyes in the photograph.

"He's in a nursing home," she says. "Sick as a dog. He ruined his liver years ago."

"He's dying?"

"He's been dying for a decade."

"Did you give him my letter?"

"What letter?"

"When we went to McDonald's."

"God, no. I tore that thing apart."

She stands and picks up her purse, adjusts the shoulder strap.

"Enough talk," she says. "I'm ready to go."

"I can't just up and leave."

"Why not?"

"I have a job. I have Maya."

"Who is with her father. This is the perfect opportunity."

"I need to think."

Amelia sighs loudly. "You've had since April to think."

"I need more time."

"Fine. You've got five minutes. Then that's it. I'm gone. I've got too many things to do to wait around for you to make up your mind."

Halfway across the room, she stops.

"You really do have a very nice life," she says. "Congratulations. Living well is no small feat."

I close my eyes, and there it is: the darkness, the unfathomable space beyond and within.

Over the years I've wondered if Robert was dead. I've wanted him to die. Not painfully. A heart attack in his sleep, a seamless slip from dream to oblivion. A peaceful exit so that part of my life could be over. That book shut.

I've never pictured him as an old man. A dying man. A collection of skin and bones collapsed in on itself, a deflated balloon in a hospital bed.

What would I say to him?

How would he see me? Who would I be standing at the foot of his bed?

The papers from Peter's lawyer still sit beside the refrigerator. I don't have to read them to know what he has begun: the slow chipping away of my relationship with my daughter. My biggest fear is that Maya will not come back from California, or if she does, she will not come back for long. Without her, I am nothing; this "nice" life of mine is nothing.

Closure, Peter would call this trip. I used to pretend I didn't need it. But I do.

"What are you doing on the floor?" Amelia says. "Are you meditating?"

"It helps me think."

She sits down next to me, crosses her legs. She positions her hands palm-up on her knees.

"Like riding a bike," she says. "Except we never learned to do that."

"My husband taught me."

"Lucky you."

She closes her eyes. After a moment, I do, too. She exhales, making a growling sound in the back of her throat, a trick Tammy taught us but which I'd forgotten. I try it and begin to feel buoyant, light.

Together we growl like tigers.

On the next inhale, I say, "I'll go."

"I never doubted you would."

I can hear the smile in her voice.

"But only if you take me to see Robert first."

I open my eyes. She keeps hers shut. Her hands form cups on her thighs, her fingers delicately curled as if holding something fragile, divine.

"You need me," I say.

Her fingers pinch together.

"All right," she says, "but I think you're out of your mind."

I almost say: You're one to talk. But I have pushed far enough. I get my coat.

two

AMELIA WRITES OUT DIRECTIONS on the back of an index card. The nursing home is outside Columbus, a two and a half hour drive.

"Give me Sara's," she says, and I remove the scrap of paper from my wallet. The trade seems fair.

In my car Amelia undresses: unzips her boots and throws them in the back; wads up her coat and stuffs it on the floor; pushes up the sleeves of her blouse. In such a closed space, I detect a sharp stench beneath her perfume—sweat and something like stale milk.

"Have you been in Ohio all this time?" I ask.

"I've been all over." With her finger, she draws a curving line in the air. "Vermont, New Hampshire, Pennsylvania, West Virginia. Here."

"Doing what?"

"Being a 'missing person,' apparently."

She brings her knees to her chest and watches the houses of my town slide by. With their porches and living rooms and kitchens lit, they make a cozy sight. Several are still festooned with Christmas decorations, ranging from classy to overly enthusiastic: small, white lights; trees wrapped in flashing bulbs; inflatable Santas and reindeer; an entire plastic nativity set in the side yard of the Delanceys. The night before Maya left, we drove down these same streets, picking out the best displays. She took pictures to show her father. "I don't know if they do this in California," she said, and I assured her they did.

"But," she said, "no snow."

"There will be plenty of snow when you get back. I guess that's not the same, though, is it?"

"Daddy says we can go swimming."

"You'd take swimming over a white Christmas?"

"Mom," she said. "There's no contest."

I drive out of town, onto the highway. Traffic is sparse, the night suddenly much darker. The flashes of light in the distance seem to belong to another planet, some unnamable star.

"Oh, look." Amelia points to a cluster of bright red lights, half-hidden by a stand of trees. On the roof, a ten-foot snowman glows. "How did they get him up there?"

"He deflates."

"Really?"

"Yeah, he's like a balloon."

"You've got to admire Midwestern earnestness," Amelia says. "I used to think about moving back here, but I'd remember that earnestness has its flipside, too."

"What's the flipside?"

"You know. A land of sheep and very few shepherds."

"New York is different?"

"It's what you make of it."

"Why did you leave?"

"I killed a man."

She leans her head against the window.

"What?"

"It's a metaphor." She raises her head and looks at me. "You're my bury-the-body friend."

"That squirrel."

"You never told on me. Ever. Well, except at the end, but those were extenuating circumstances. We'll call it a one-off. Confused allegiance. Adolescence. Whatever. You were good at keeping my secrets. Good at protecting me."

She pulls her coat over her body.

"Believing me," she says.

"Did you make up Sara's address?"

"Do you mean did I write it myself?"

"Yeah," I say, realizing the stupidity of the question, the contradiction to what she just said.

"No," Amelia says.

I focus on the glow of the headlights. I've taken the highway to Columbus dozens of times, most recently shopping for school clothes with Maya. We ate lunch at a restaurant known for their French fries. That's all we ate, with glasses of too sweet raspberry iced tea, dunking the fries in ketchup and barbeque sauce. Grease coated our fingers and lips. We had been two girls, out on the town, trying on funny hats, buying sparkly belts, singing along to the radio.

Amelia shifts, pulling her coat tighter around her shoulders, and I notice again the stench beneath her perfume.

The bury-the-body friend. The title disturbs me, makes me proud. Stalwart, I think. Strong. Out of all the nameless, faceless people in her life, I am the one she's come to.

"You'd be mine," I say.

She doesn't respond.

"Except I don't have any bodies. Not that many."

"Your ex-husband," she says.

"Husband. And he can't be a body. We have Maya."

"Robert."

I turn on the radio. Without looking, Amelia reaches over and turns it off.

"If we find Sara," I say, "will you stay in Chicago?"

"That depends on her answers to my questions. Now if you don't mind, I'm going to try to sleep for a bit. Slap me if you need me to drive."

✳

THE NURSING HOME IS oblong, modern, white siding and glass, lit by parking lot lights, right where Amelia said it would be. It reminds me of Glory's condominium, sleek, antiseptic, a step into the future. Funny they would both end up in places like this, as far away as you could get from log cabins and composting toilets.

The lot is almost empty; it's nearly one o'clock. I pull into a space directly in front of the doors. When I turn off the engine, Amelia stirs.

"We're here," I say, and she grunts. I put my hand on her shoulder.

"Go without me," she says, her voice garbled by sleep.

I hesitate, then open the door and step out into the cold, windless night.

The doors to the building are locked. I begin to panic before I notice a button to the side and press it. After a moment, I hear a soft click and the door gives beneath my push.

Behind a curved counter sits a woman Glory's age, her chin resting on her hand. She wears pale blue scrubs, her red hair pulled back in a ponytail, dark roots showing.

"Yes?" she says, sitting up straight.

"I'm here to see Robert Holbrook."

"Honey, it's the middle of the night."

The clock above her head reads one-ten. "I know it's a little late," I say.

"Visiting hours ended at nine."

"I'm sorry. I tried to get here sooner. I've been traveling all day, and my car broke down."

"And you are?"

"His daughter. Sara Holbrook."

The lie is instantaneous, instinctual. As soon as I've said it, I know it was the right move.

"I came all the way from Chicago," I say.

"Let her see him, Deb."

A young woman, also dressed in scrubs, these ones covered in smiling cartoon children, stands at the far end of the lobby, beneath an oval mirror.

"I just checked on him," she says, "and he's awake. I'm sure he'd like the company."

Deb pushes a binder toward me and gestures toward the page. "Name and time," she says, her eyes heavy, already bored with me.

I begin to write my own name and stop, turning the C into an awkward S.

The young nurse waits for me.

"I'm Jess," she says. "Your dad's on my night list."

"How is he?"

"Holding on. He's got insomnia. Most nights he stays up playing solitaire. I've tried to give him sleeping aides, but he won't take them. He doesn't bother anyone so." She shrugs. "He's lucky he's got me. Some of the other nurses wouldn't let him off so easy."

We walk down a long, dimly lit corridor that reminds me of a middle-grade hotel, the carpet beige, the walls a slightly darker tan, the doors identical save for a few decorated with holiday wreaths, strands of bells, American flag stickers, crayon drawings.

Glory's parents, the only set of grandparents I knew, died the year after we moved out of their house in Cleveland. He went first, a heart attack. She followed seven months later. "Lovesick," I once said to Glory, but she wouldn't let me be romantic. "She stopped taking her pills," Glory said. "She ate everything her doctor told her not to. Cakes, doughnuts, ice cream, sherry. She wanted to die, but she wanted to go out happy."

Both ways seem better than slow death in this anonymous place. I want to ask Jess how long Robert has been here, but his daughter—a daughter who would visit him, a fake daughter—would know.

"Here we are," Jess says, knocking lightly while opening the door.

I follow, almost tripping on her heels.

The room is larger than I expected, a curtain separating it in half. Ten feet from us a man snores in his bed. He looks like any other old man, but Jess keeps moving. She steps around the curtain.

In a wheelchair next to the window, Robert sits upright, his spine as straight as ever, his hair wispy, his skin old leather, Tammy's skin. He wears a gray flannel bathrobe, faded yellow pajamas, white slippers. The outfit, more than anything else, strikes me as undignified, beneath him.

Tears press against the back of my eyes, and I close them, absorbing, and take another look.

On the windowsill are cards, lit by a desk lamp, but he isn't looking at them. He is looking at us, our reflection in the window.

"Your daughter's here," Jess says brightly. "Sara."

She brings over what looks like a kitchen chair and places it beside him.

"Sara," he says, still watching me in the window.

His voice is the same and isn't. His voice, but hole-ridden. Moth-eaten.

"She came all the way from Chicago," Jess says.

I sit down. "Hi," I say.

He looks at the cards.

Jess places her hands on Robert's still-broad shoulders. "Push the button when you get tired," she says.

She leaves us on our own. Behind the curtain, the man's snore breaks. He gasps for air, and my body tenses. There is silence, and then he snores again.

Robert turns over a card. The four of clubs.

"Sara," he says, and I wonder if his mind has gone, if he thinks I really am Sara. His blue eyes are rheumy, but they still pierce, hold me in place.

I shouldn't have come.

"Why Sara?" he says.

"Since I'm not a blood relative," I say, "I wasn't sure they'd let me in."

"Blood relative. Is there another kind?"

Before I can reply, he says, "Why not Amelia?"

"She's in the car."

"Is she?" He sits back, hands dangling over his lap. "She and I aren't on very good terms. It's not her fault."

"I'm here," I say.

"She murdered me in her poems."

"I didn't read those."

"I was between the lines, but I was there." He nods slowly. "I saw myself. I knew what was going on. And I deserved it. I'm not claiming otherwise."

"I'm here," I say again, and add, "Carrie."

"Carrie," he says. "I would have thought you'd have forgotten about me."

"How could I forget?"

He tries to snap his fingers, but they make no sound. "A blip," he says, "in a long life."

"A blip? You and Amelia were my childhood."

He tucks his chin into his chest, closes his eyes. The seconds pass, and I begin to think he's fallen asleep. Half standing, I reach out to shake him awake.

He looks up at me from beneath his eyelids.

"You want my apology," he says.

I hover, my hand inches away from his shoulder. My body falls back and lands on the chair with a thud.

"No," I say. "I just came to see you."

But that isn't true, exactly.

"I've apologized in my heart I don't know how many times," he says. "I've apologized to God."

"God?"

"But that's not the same. I understand that. I was a sinner back then and I only got worse."

"I didn't view you that way."

"You were a good girl," he says.

I am growing impatient. There has been too much talking in circles tonight, too much in my lifetime. I decide to get on with it.

"Why did you leave Orion?" I say.

Robert lifts his dangling hands. They hang in the air like puppets. "I had to. I was ruining Amelia's life. I was ruining yours. It was all on the point of blowing up." He flicks his fingers, simulating an explosion. "Best for everyone to leave."

"You should have told me."

"What could I have said to make it any easier? I left you with your parents, where you belonged."

"No," I say. "I didn't belong."

"Where would you have been better off?"

His gaze makes me uncomfortable. I look at his legs in the yellow flannel pajama bottoms, his feet in the cheap white slippers.

"Is Sara alive or dead?" I say.

"She might as well be dead."

"What does that mean?"

He leans forward, and I do, too, ready to grab him if he falls from his chair.

"She runs off at fifteen." His voice low, tight with anger. "Shows up at my house seven months later with a newborn. Takes off again. And again. And again. She wouldn't have been any kind of good influence on Amelia. We both decided—"

"That she would be dead."

Robert swivels his wheelchair to the right, toward his bed. "It was the right thing to do," he says. "The least complicated outcome."

"For who?"

"Better to think her mother dead than didn't want her."

"Is Sara still alive? Is she in Chicago?"

He gives his chair another push, away from me. "Leave her alone," he says. "We've made peace with that."

"We?"

"You shouldn't go unearthing what's buried. It's been buried for a reason."

"You mean like me coming here?"

His arms frustrate him. He starts scooting toward his bed using his feet.

There is nothing more to say.

I embrace him. He feels small, a child in my arms. He does not smell like himself: there's a bland, astringent aftershave and, beneath, the faint scent of urine. He does not lift his arms, but he pats my hand, once.

"Take care of my girl," he says, and I think I hear a catch in his voice. He clears his throat, and I wonder if I only imagined—only wanted—a stray remnant of sorrow. Of missing me.

I push him to his bed. He picks up a remote lying on the mattress, and waits for the nurse with his back to me, as if I have already gone.

Jess is coming down the hall.

"Thank you," I say.

"Not easy, is it?"

I shake my head.

Jess puts her hand on my forearm.

"Whatever he tells you," she says, "he appreciates having you here."

three

AMELIA DOESN'T STIR AS I pull out of the parking lot and navigate my way onto the highway. I consider waking her and decide not to; I don't know how much to tell her yet.

It's not even two. I was with Robert less than half an hour.

To stay awake, I roll down the window. The cold air feels good. Driving feels good. I have always enjoyed driving at night: the otherworldly glow of headlights, lives glimpsed through windows, the illusion of being apart, outside of time and place. Sometimes Peter and I would go for nighttime drives. To Cleveland, through deserted streets, chasing neon signs. To Lake Erie, to sneak onto the shore and watch the waves. Or even just through our town, searching for hidden beauty inside the familiar, finding it in a late night train rumbling over the tracks, an old man and woman sitting on their porch, a young mother pushing a stroller across the parking lot of the 7-Eleven. On these drives Peter and I would rarely speak. We would just look at each other and know that we were experiencing something valuable. Something we thought would be lasting.

Beside me Amelia sleeps like a baby.

I'm afraid that when we reach Chicago, we will find an empty apartment. The door will swing on its hinges. Dirt and paper will blow in through the broken windows. Glass will litter the floor. I will follow Amelia through the rooms, calling Sara's name. We will open the closets, the kitchen cupboards, just in case she has shrunken down in size. We will come up with nothing—not even a lock of hair, a flake of skin, a fingernail, a whitened bone.

I step on the gas. We are on a rescue mission now, a long way left to go.

✳

As WE CROSS OVER into Indiana, I turn on the radio for company. The DJ's name is Delilah, her weightless voice hypnotic.

"This next song is for Marjory from Rick," she says, "who is finishing up his tour of duty in Afghanistan. He wants Marjory to remember the roller coaster in Palm Springs. 'Honey,' he says, 'I'll be home soon, and I'm going to take you for another ride.'"

Louis Armstrong's "What A Wonderful World." A song that makes Glory cry. I see them, Rick and Marjory, the happy young couple from a television ad, riding together into the sky, all of their heartache and fear discarded in a tangled heap below.

On a stream of easy listening dedicated from one aching, celebrating soul to another, Delilah carries me through the night. Eric Clapton marks an engagement, Paula Cole a sister who has moved away. I make up faces for Tim in Omaha, Nancy in St. Louis, Laura in St. Petersburg, Ben in Pleasantville. They pile into the backseat with their fresh faces, their easy joviality and everyday pain. I want to be one of them. I would dedicate Crosby, Stills, Nash, and Young's "Our House" to Peter, followed by Leonard Cohen's "The Stranger Song," to solidify my point. For Robert, I'd make a request for Bob Dylan's "Girl from the North Country," a song Glory bought on tape after we left Orion and sometimes played in the long hours after dinner or on weekend mornings while I was still in bed. She told me it had been one of Mike's favorite songs in college, and I understood that by playing it, she was sending out a call, hoping somewhere he'd hear and come back to her, like a lost dog or a child whose hand she'd let go of in the grocery store, returning remorseful and relieved.

Peter and Robert would never understand. They would listen

to the songs and hear only the words, the melody. They wouldn't recognize me there, naked inside the notes.

✳

At six o'clock in the morning, Delilah bids us goodbye. I'm not ready for her to go. I scan the radio stations, but she has vanished, replaced by early morning traffic reports, country songs, Mozart, a man with a reedy voice praising Jesus.

I retreat into the silence, debating which song I'd send to Maya. When she was a baby, I used to rock her to sleep with the usual lullabies, but sometimes I'd throw in the Beatles' "Maxwell's Silver Hammer" just for the fun of it. I liked the dark humor of the song, the irony of the upbeat tempo. Watching from the nursery doorway, Peter would shake his head and laugh.

"You'll give that kid a complex," he'd say, but he didn't try to stop me.

The song now strikes me as grotesque. What nightmarish images did I plant in her infant brain—silver hammers crashing down on innocent skulls, serial killers evading the law, forever getting the upper hand? If I had been less interested in fun and more concerned about justice, maybe Maya would be a more carefree child, her burdens carried by me instead of her.

I wish I knew what her bed in California looks like, what color the sheets are, how many pillows. When she was a newborn Peter didn't know what to do with her. He held her stiffly, afraid of dropping. "She's not made of glass," I'd say, overly critical so that he would hand her back to me.

For almost a year I'd taken my basal body temperature every morning, tracked my ovulation on the kitchen calendar. We took vitamins by the handful, and when my period came, I felt a deep, personal shame. When I finally became pregnant, we held our breath through the first trimester in desperate fear that something would go wrong.

I didn't want drugs.

"You'll change your mind," Glory said.

"At least keep the option open," Peter said.

I wrote my wishes down on a piece of paper, which I signed and made Peter witness.

I said, "Natural childbirth is beautiful."

And, "I want to be fully present and connected."

And, "Women have been doing this since the dawn of time."

What I meant was: I want the pain to overwhelm me; I want the pain to become me. I want to be at the mercy of my daughter so that I will understand how to be a mother.

I understood so little.

The hormones erased my memory. Nature's life preserver, Peter called it. I don't know how long I was in labor or how many people were in the room. All I know is that one moment Maya was not part of the world, and the next moment she was and that was when our life began.

My-a. Mine.

"I'm coming," I whisper. "Hold on, mi amour. I'm coming."

four

As we enter Gary, Indiana, the sky grows light and the highway clogs with traffic. I slam on my breaks, sending Amelia tumbling forward. She sits up, blinking, her hair in disarray.

"Where are we?" She wrinkles her nose. "God, it's freezing." She stares at me until I close my window. All sound disappears but the hum of the motor, giving the impression that we have been sealed off, or the world has.

"We're getting close," I say. "There's a map in the side pocket. You're going to have to guide me."

The paper crinkles as Amelia unfolds the map.

"Come here often?" she says, and I glance over, at my yellow highlighted routes.

"Once," I say. "Family vacation."

"Any Sara sightings?"

"That wasn't the point."

"I'm kidding. You take everything too seriously. You always have." She folds the map into crisp quarters. "How was Robert?"

"Asleep."

"The whole time?"

"Most of it. When he was awake, he wasn't very coherent."

"Born again," she says. "Did he tell you that?"

"Not in so many words."

"Praise the lord."

"I thought you said he was a drunk."

"Those traits aren't mutually exclusive. He repented everything except his drinking. You were at the top of his list."

"Why me?" I say.

"Don't pretend, Carrie. I know what went on between you two. He told me, but I should have seen the signs while it was happening. Guess I was too preoccupied with my own Prince Charming."

I look straight ahead, at back of a semi-truck, the yellow warning sign for wide turns.

"He found God and the bottle at just about the same time," Amelia says. "Both made his lips slick. All his secrets came tumbling out. Except for Sara. He's stuck to that old lie."

"Did he?" I say. "To you?"

"No. For a while I thought it meant he loved you more. Or you loved him more. I resented you both. How's that for twisted? You were a child." Her voice softens. "We both were."

I spot an opening and speed up, jerking the steering wheel to the left. Our bodies are thrust forward and back. The driver of the truck that I've cut off lays on his horn. In the rearview mirror, I see him flick me off.

"Nice handling," Amelia says.

I blow my hair out of my face.

"Why did you go with him?" I say. "Why didn't you come get me?"

"Jesus, Carrie," Amelia says. "What choice did I have? Anyway, I wasn't thinking about you right then. I just wanted to get away from Orion. You had Glory and Mike. You weren't alone."

But I was.

Sitting on Robert's porch.

Lying beneath him in the woods.

Tearing apart the vegetable garden.

Listening to Glory cry.

I was alone.

"I wouldn't have left you," I say.

"That's bullshit."

"No, it's the truth. You were everything to me."

"See," Amelia says, "that's a problem. I was fourteen. I couldn't be expected to carry you. I had my own life to worry about."

"I carried *you*," I say. "I kept *your* secrets. And you wouldn't let me go. All those postcards. You haven't let me move on."

"What do you want me to say? I'm sorry?"

"No. I don't know. What about 'thank you'?"

"All right," Amelia says flatly. "Thank you."

I am hunched over the steering wheel, breathing hard.

"You'd rather not be here," she says.

The space between my shoulder blades throbs.

"Did I have a choice?" I say.

"Free will."

I can't tell if she's being sarcastic or not.

After a while she tells me to get in the right lane.

✳

CHICAGO IS AS I remembered it, only now I am not a passive observer but the one behind the wheel. I meet and exceed the aggression of the city drivers, taking risks I never would back home. Meanwhile, Amelia stares wide-eyed out the window, her hands clasped in her lap like an obedient child, as we leave the highway for commercial thoroughfares, turning down tree-lined boulevards, coming at last to quiet side streets of brick townhouses, greystone apartment buildings.

On the sidewalk an older woman with a severe bob and a puffy, purple coat pauses as her terrier sniffs the base of a lamppost. Amelia twists in her seat to keep the woman in view.

When we are a few blocks from Sara's street, Amelia tells me to stop.

"I need coffee," she says. "And a bathroom."

I circle the block twice before finding a parking space. As I slide in, I bump the car behind me. I pull forward and knock into the car in front.

"It's too small," I say.

Amelia opens her door. "We're fine."

"I'm sticking way out."

"Can we just go?" She slams the door behind her. When I join her on the street, she is trying to light a cigarette, but her hands are shaking. I take the lighter from her. "Thank God," she says.

My breath curls up beside Amelia's cigarette smoke. Despite the bright sunlight, the air has the crystallized feel of approaching snow. I stuff my hands in my pockets, stamp my feet, but Amelia takes her time, staring up at the sky as she smokes down to the stub.

We find a coffee shop. Amelia rushes to the restroom while I order our drinks and, as an afterthought, two blueberry scones. Although I have not eaten in over twelve hours, the sight of the scone on its little white plate nauseates me. I break it into bite size pieces and force my jaw to move, my throat to swallow. My body catches on to what it's supposed to do, and I recognize that the scone tastes good—buttery, the blueberry flavor sharp. I eat Amelia's scone, too, and go up to the counter for two more.

By the time Amelia comes back from the restroom, I am halfway through with my third scone.

"Are these vegan?" she says.

"No. You're still doing that?"

"You're not?"

"We stopped when we left."

She pushes the plate toward me. "I couldn't eat anyway."

I wrap the scone in a napkin and put it in my purse for later, something I would never do under ordinary circumstances. But we are very far from ordinary. I don't know what to expect, what provisions I might need.

Amelia bends over her coffee, looking the part of an invalid in an old movie—exhausted and weak but possessing an otherworldly glamour that would make even the healthiest person envious. Her eyes seem to have grown several sizes and now swim in their sockets as she peers around the coffee shop, taking in the overweight man in the suit checking his cell phone screen in the corner; the old man in the fedora carefully spreading cream cheese on his bagel; the young couple by the window, sharing one cup between them. At the counter, a girl with green streaked hair chats with a boy with a stud between his eyebrows. Amelia's gaze lingers on them.

"What do you hope to find?" I say, breaking her trance. She blows on her coffee.

"My mother," she says.

"But what will that change? What will it prove?"

"Maybe nothing. Maybe everything. Why did you want to see Robert?"

"Closure," I say.

"Exactly. You know, Orion wouldn't have existed without Robert and me."

"Tammy—"

"Wouldn't have been able to do it on her own. Before you guys came, before Meg and Calvin, it was just the three of us. We were the bedrock. Without us Orion would have failed within a year, and your family never would have moved there. You would've had a happy, normal childhood."

"Not with my parents."

"Who's to say? They might have been completely different people without the stresses of that place."

"That's too many what-ifs."

"Until we meet Sara, that's all we've got."

"Even after."

"Sure. But at least we'll be able to look her in the face. At least we'll know whether she's alive or dead."

Before I can reply, Amelia is on her feet.

"Do you know Sara Holbrook?" she says, directing the question to the girl behind the counter but speaking loudly enough for the whole coffee shop to hear.

"Sara what?"

"Holbrook, I think. She lives around here."

"What does she look like?"

"Like me."

"I don't think so," the girl says. "Do you know anyone, Thomas?"

"Sorry," the boy says.

Amelia turns on her heels and walks out.

I should follow her, but my coffee is only half drunk, my body desperate for rest. I feel myself sinking farther into the old-fashioned metal chair, the type they used to use in ice cream parlors. My muscles ache as if I have run all the way from Ohio.

I lift my mug, put it back down, sloshing hot coffee over my fingers. Just out of sight Amelia waits for me. I sense her impatience; it gnaws at the pit of my stomach. I can't not follow.

five

I **FIND HER SMOKING** on the corner.

"About time," she says and crosses the street.

I trail behind. Every once in a while I see her shoulders tense, her head move almost imperceptibly to the right as she tries to catch me in her peripheral vision, making sure I am still there. As children, she never felt the need to look back. I find myself slowing my step and then, feeling guilty, speed up until we are side by side.

"Here we are," she says.

The buildings on Harper Avenue are understated, tidy, the sidewalks clear. At the end of the block, bundled up children run in a fenced-in schoolyard, their shouts amplified by the morning stillness. As we watch, an electronic bell sounds and the children bump into each other as they make their way inside.

Amelia takes the scrap of paper from her pocket, although I know she must have the address memorized. I do.

She starts down the block, holding the paper up to each building we pass, as if the numbers may have suddenly changed, or are continuously evolving. She stops so abruptly that I almost run into her. We both look at the paper, confirming the gold numbers beside the door of this brownstone. I look up at the second floor, but wooden shutters block the windows.

"It'll be like seeing a ghost," I say, and Amelia gives me an irritated look. But a ghost is now what I expect—whether alive or dead, a spectral figure dressed in white, with cold hands, a musical voice, the ability to walk through walls. Anything less extraordinary will be a disappointment.

The name slot beside the buzzer for 2B is empty.

I start laughing.

"Stop it," Amelia hisses.

"I can't," I say, the words unintelligible. I sit down on the steps and double over, my stomach cramping. Amelia nudges me in the spine with her foot.

"What is wrong with you?" she says.

I lift my head and look out at the deserted street. No one knows where I am; I have successfully slipped away with Amelia as we had planned all those years ago, as if we were responsible only for each other. But we're not. I'm not.

I take out my cell phone. No new messages have come in, but Maya would have slept through our journey. She would be waking up right about now.

"Are you going to do this or not?" Amelia says.

I wipe my eyes on my sleeve. It's improbable, unthinkable, yet somehow, here I am.

Here we are.

Amelia presses the buzzer for 2A, the apartment next door to Sara. We wait for what seems an eternity.

Could this be a building full of abandoned apartments? Are we waiting for voices long ago extinct?

But there is the crackle and an old woman saying, "Who's there?"

Amelia leans in close, speaking loudly and smoothly, Robert's solicitous tone.

"Good morning," she says. "So sorry to disturb you. We're looking for Sara Holbrook in 2B, but she isn't answering."

"This isn't 2B."

"I know, but—"

"You've rung the wrong place."

"Yes, you see— "

The door clicks.

Amelia leads the way into a dimly lit foyer that smells of cats.

She pauses in front of the mailboxes lining the left wall. "Look," she says, clicking her nails on the box for 2B. The rusty nameplate reads *SH.*

The stairs moan. Halfway up Amelia lets out a squeal and jumps to the side as a fat yellow cat pushes past.

The door to 2B is just an ordinary door.

As Amelia knocks, I am back at Mosey Inn, standing beside Robert as he knocks on the door to room nine. Irrationally, I think that Amelia at fourteen will be inside, and when she sees me, I will become fourteen, too.

Time is occurring wrong again; I am in and out of sequence.

"She isn't home."

At the end of the hall a tiny woman with stringy gray hair stands in the doorway of 2A, cradling a black kitten. She wears a blue flannel housecoat and dirty white slippers that remind me of the ones Robert was wearing at the nursing home.

"We're looking for Sara," Amelia says.

"Yes, yes, I heard you before. She isn't home."

"But she does live here?"

The woman sighs. "I've told you that."

"Do you know when she'll be back?"

"Oh, Lord knows. She's like that, Sara. She's, what-do-they-call-it, a free spirit. Doesn't like to be tied to one place. A wanderer."

"Where does she wander?"

The woman waves in the direction of the street. "All over. Even on days like this, with snow coming. I tell her she'll catch cold and die. Freeze on the sidewalk. Happens every year. But she doesn't listen."

"Do you know when she'll be back?"

The kitten squirms. Without bending, the woman drops it. It lands on its feet but teeters for a moment before retreating swaybacked into the apartment.

"Who's asking?" the woman says.

"Her daughter."

"Sara doesn't have a daughter. She's got no family."

"Actually," Amelia says, "she does."

"Is that a fact?" Stepping into the hallway, the woman removes a pair of glasses from the pocket of her housecoat. The red plastic frames take up her entire face. "These damn lights," she says. "They don't replace the bulbs."

"But you see a resemblance?" Amelia says.

"Can't hardly tell." The woman looks at me. "And who's this? Another daughter?"

"A friend," Amelia says.

"Two lost daughters, showing up out of the blue." Shaking her head, the woman takes off her glasses and snaps the frames shut. "Seems a little fishy to me."

"Why would we lie?" Amelia says. "What could we possibly be after?"

"Lord knows. The world today."

"Is just like the world yesterday and the day before and the day before."

"Maybe so," the woman says. "Maybe so." She places her hands on her hips and angles her chin up, looking from Amelia to me, and back again. "I can't just leave you out here, and if I tell you to go, I doubt you'll listen. Is that about right?"

"You've got it," Amelia says.

"All right, then. Would you ladies like a cup of tea?"

Without waiting for a response, the woman goes back inside her apartment, closing the door behind her.

"What do we do now?" I say.

"We go in," Amelia says, "and have tea."

The door has been left on its latch, but Amelia knocks anyway.

"Open," the woman yells.

We enter a studio, the walls and floor bright yellow, like we're stepping into the sun. At the center of the room the woman sits at a folding table, the kitten in her lap. Behind her, on a twin mattress, sleeps a tangled mass of cats.

"I've only got one extra chair," the woman says. "One of you will have to kneel."

Amelia gestures for me to take the chair, but I shake my head. This moment is more hers than mine.

"I'm Marybeth," the woman says. "Thanks for asking."

"Sorry," Amelia says, but Marybeth swats the air. The kitten lifts its paw, mimicking the gesture.

Marybeth pours tea from a pale yellow teapot, spotted with age, into three porcelain cups decorated with ivy.

"Careful," she says. "These are hand painted. Mother's."

The teacup feels as thin as an eggshell; I'm sure I will break it. I take a small sip and set it back on the table.

"How long have you known Sara?" Amelia asks.

"Since she moved in, oh, what, thirty, forty years ago?"

"She's been here that whole time?"

"Not here, here. She's had this address, sure, but like I said, she's a free spirit. A wanderer. Not me. I'm a homebody. I've got these rascals to look after."

"When she's not here," Amelia says, "where is she?"

"She usually stays at St. Brigid's."

"St. Brigid's?"

"The mission. Says they've got the best bedding in town and good food, too."

"You mean a homeless shelter?"

"A nice one," Marybeth says.

Amelia looks at me. "Why would she go to a homeless shelter?"

"Who knows?" Marybeth stands, the kitten clinging to her housecoat, riding along for several steps before falling to the floor. She opens the cupboard above the kitchen sink and takes down a loaf of bread. "I guess she likes the adventure."

My knees ache. I shift until I am sitting cross-legged, my eyes at table height.

"Can you give us directions to St. Brigid's?" Amelia says.

Marybeth stuffs a piece of bread in her mouth and takes out another, wads it up in her fist. "Kitties," she calls, singsong, and tosses the ball of bread onto the mattress, right into the middle of the pile of cats. They spring to life, backs arched, tails raised. "Look at them!" she cries, pointing.

"Marybeth," Amelia says.

"Yeah, yeah, the directions. I'll give them to you on one condition." She places her hand on her heart, all merriment gone from her face. "You better not let on they came from me."

"We won't tell her."

"Promise."

"We promise," I say.

Marybeth looks at Amelia.

"Promise," Amelia says.

"On your mother's life," Marybeth says.

"Sure," Amelia says. "On Sara's life."

"You break that promise, I'll hunt you down. I'm not as nice as I look. And neither is Sara."

"We believe you," I say.

Marybeth takes a crumpled receipt from her pocket. "One of you daughters got a pen?"

six

"INSANE," AMELIA SAYS, BUT we are on a city bus, following Marybeth's directions downtown to St. Bridgid's. Squeezed into the tight seats, I cannot distinguish the smell of Amelia's sweat and unwashed hair from mine, and that fact both pleases and disturbs me. I am aware of the threat of going backwards, of becoming again two halves of a whole.

"Marybeth isn't insane," I say. "She's lonely."

I use my sleeve to wipe away a circle in the fogged up window. Snow has begun to fall, but the flakes are sparse, graceful in their singularity. On the sidewalk only a few people rush with bent heads. The rest walk with the nonchalance of those used to heavy snow and harsh winds, who consider a snowflake or two in January to be good weather, worthy even of a lunchtime stroll.

I have not been in a big city in years. I've barely even been to Cleveland. I work on the outskirts, in a commercial park built thirty years ago, the buildings uniformly ugly with their straight gray lines and tinted windows. Everyone drives in and drives out, home to the suburbs, without ever brushing shoulders with a stranger. Lunches are eaten at our desks or at one of the fast food restaurants lining the highway. On the rare occasions the department hosts a happy hour, we go to the fake Irish pub, where the waitresses wear t-shirts emblazoned with the franchise's name, made available to patrons for thirty-five dollars; we can also buy pint glasses, shot glasses, alarm clocks, even a teddy bear wearing the t-shirt (I bought one for Maya), all for astronomical prices. We order the same hamburgers and beers, which we pretend are the epitome of their kind, that we can get at the identical pub in the suburban sprawl where we live or any place we might travel. Familiarity is comfort we take for granted, no longer even noticed, like love or good health.

We are such perfect specimens of SAS.

A life lived in the city, simultaneously and at cross-purposes with so many others, would be exhilarating. As one among several million, you'd have to carve out your space. You'd have to guard and defend as other identities pressed in from all sides, threatening to break down your boundaries, pour in, wash over you, carry you away.

Here, you'd have to grow strong and stay strong.

I watch Amelia watching an old woman seated at the front of the bus. The woman wears a bright pink hat, a matching brocade coat and gloves. She sits erect with her head held high, her hands folded on top of her metal cane.

"The city isn't a place to grow old," Amelia says.

"Why not?"

"You get lost."

The woman in pink presses the button for the next stop.

"She seems to know where she's going," I say.

"I'm not talking about her. I'm talking about me."

Amelia looks down at the grocery receipt on which Marybeth has scrawled the directions to the mission. Marybeth's handwriting is beautifully archaic, the sort of ornate cursive practiced by girls generations ago, too old even for Marybeth. Her mother, owner of the hand painted teacups, must have taught her. I imagine a strict woman with tightly coiled hair. In another time and place, I would mention this vision to Amelia and let her take the story from there. But now I want to separate; I need to test myself. I enlarge the scene, giving Marybeth's mother a cameo brooch and green eyes, a youthful face and swanlike neck. Her long fingers point out the mistakes: the way the letters slope in the wrong direction here, the laziness of the *t* over there.

Maya would appreciate such a lady, like a character from an L.M. Montgomery novel.

I take out my cell phone. Amelia grabs it.

"What are you doing?"

She puts my phone in her purse. "You need to be with me," she says.

"My daughter might call."

"Nothing is so important it can't wait."

"Only this."

"This has been forty years in the making. More. This has been coming since the dawn of time."

I wish I could argue with her, but I can't.

✳

St. Brigid's Mission occupies a narrow brick building between a storefront church and a vacant lot whose chain link fence has been knocked in, as if rammed by a car. The door to the mission is propped open with a plastic milk crate, and Amelia and I go inside, down a short hall smelling of onions and disinfectant. At the end is a window, above which hang a large wooden cross and a painting of a woman in a dark shroud, a golden light encircling her head. Her beatific expression reminds me of Joan of Arc's, and I find my mouth forming the same knowing smile. It feels nice, like slipping back into a favorite outfit even though you know the look is outdated, the fit never quite right to begin with.

The window has a small, mesh opening at the right height to speak into if you stoop, but no one sits at the messy desk inside. On the wall is a black button, which Amelia pushes again and again until someone appears.

I had hoped for a nun in a wimple and habit, but this woman wears jeans and a sweatshirt decorated with snowmen. Snowman earrings dangle from her ears. Her face is plain, her hair thinning and tightly curled.

"Have you come to volunteer?" she asks with a big smile and

Minnesotan twang.

"We're looking for someone," Amelia says. "She stays here sometimes."

The woman's smile disappears.

"Her name is Sara Holbrook."

"And who might be asking?"

"Her daughter."

"She isn't here right now. All residents have to clear out at nine. They can come back for lunch at one and return for dinner and a bed at seven."

"But you are certain that she comes here?" Amelia says. "Her name is Sara Holbrook."

"I know of several Saras," the woman says.

"Can you check your records?"

"We protect our women's privacy, for everyone's safety. I'm sure you must understand."

"I'm not here to do her harm."

"Honey," the woman says, "I'm sure you're not, but I'm not about to betray a trust. Come back at one and we'll see if we can't find her."

"Thank you," I say. "We'll do that."

I take Amelia by the elbow and guide her down the hall, out onto the street.

"It's like a quest," I say.

"What?"

"Obstacles in our path. Guards. Tests of our endurance."

"Right."

"Sara is the holy grail."

"We don't know that yet," Amelia says.

The wind has picked up and with it the snow. Our hair whips across our faces, and I let go of Amelia and zip my coat all the way up.

At half past twelve, the women start arriving. They show up alone, in groups of two or three, some wearing coats and hats and gloves, others with chapped hands, their bodies wrapped in blankets. One pulls along a shopping cart piled high with plastic bags of tin cans. Many have backpacks, a few children who race each other back and forth along the sidewalk. A woman with hair cropped close to her head pushes a baby stroller, the passenger a radio playing hip-hop.

With every new arrival, Amelia's posture stiffens; as she scans the woman's face, hers lights up. I look, too. Many of the women are the right age, but none of the features add up, none even close.

At one o'clock the woman in the snowman sweatshirt steps outside with two teenagers wearing white aprons and carrying clipboards. "Good afternoon, ladies," she says as the women form a ragtag line to the right of the door.

"Sister Madge," the woman with the stroller shouts, "we're freezing our asses off."

"You'll be inside in a minute."

As the women file past, Sister Madge spots us.

"Any luck?"

Amelia shakes her head.

"It was Sara what?"

"Holbrook."

Sister Madge steps into the middle of the sidewalk and, cupping her hands around her mouth, calls out to the line, "If Sara Holbrook is here, these two ladies would like to say hello. If Sara's not here and you know her, please be so kind as to pass along the message."

A few heads turn in our direction, but no one approaches.

"Don't worry," Madge says. "There are always stragglers."

Amelia points to the clipboards. "Can we see those?"

"I'm afraid not, honey. They wouldn't be much use anyhow. We get a lot of fake names here. Or names different from what you might know her by."

"Can we go in?" I ask.

Sister Madge studies us. After a moment, she says, "I don't see why not."

The cafeteria is on the second floor, up a flight of metal stairs that echo with each footfall. Sea green tiles cover the floor and walls, reminding me of an indoor swimming pool. Even the air is similarly humid, although most of the women keep their coats on. The tables are like those in Maya's school lunchroom, long and foldable with round stools attached. Children's artwork decorates the walls: construction paper snowflakes, crayon drawings of Santa and the nativity, traces of hands layered together to form a Christmas tree, foil presents underneath. The effect is surreal; I half-expect to see Shirley Benson and the other room mothers in white aprons, serving up bowls of soup.

Amelia and I thread our way through the tables. The women at the front have their heads bent over their food while the ones in the back wait patiently to be served. Only a few speak, but their voices bounce off the tile surfaces, becoming a multitude. A baby cries and is quickly soothed.

We take a seat at the empty end of the most sparsely populated table, where we have a good view of the door. Amelia cannot sit still. She folds her arms, places her elbows on the table, rests her chin in her hand, runs her hands through her hair. This jitteriness is new, and I wonder when she acquired it, what happened to the girl who could sit quietly for hours watching for deer.

"A needle in a haystack," she says, crossing and uncrossing her legs. "What's she doing out here when she has a home?"

"A free spirit," I say.

"Just like me," Amelia says. "Just like Robert. Only worse."

Turning her back to me, she slides down the seats until she is beside a woman with graying dreadlocks. "Excuse me?" she says, and the woman looks up, her spoon halfway to her mouth.

"You're the one looking?" the woman says.

"Yes, do you know Sara?"

The woman pours the soup from her spoon back into her bowl. "Can't say I do."

"There's a lot at stake in finding her."

"That's nice," the woman says. "Real nice."

"But it doesn't change your answer?"

The woman pushes back from the table. "You calling me a liar?"

"Please," Amelia says. "I never would."

Their eyes remain locked. Slowly the dreadlocked woman

lowers her gaze. Her shoulders round, her head bends over her food, closing Amelia off.

But Amelia is undeterred. She moves on, crouching beside the next woman's seat. I can't hear what she's saying, but I imagine that smooth, solicitous voice. I never could perfect it; I never had the patience. I wonder if that voice would have dispelled some of my worst moments with Peter. Probably not.

"Here you are, honey." Madge plops a cardboard box in front of me. "Time to use those hands of yours."

She shows me how to situate a plastic spoon, fork, and knife at an angle on a paper napkin, roll the napkin up, and close the bundle with a rubber band.

"It's not fancy," she says, but I try to make each bundle nice. I redo the first one four times before I'm satisfied. After I've made five bundles, I look up and see that Amelia has progressed to the other side of the room.

I go back to my work.

"Hey. You're supposed to be helping me." Amelia pulls the bundle out of my hand and taps me on the shoulder. "You look tired," she says.

"I haven't slept."

"You will. We're getting closer. I can feel her, can't you?"

But Sara is not at the next table, or the next.

At the third, a woman with a shock of red hair and a narrow face like a fox's says, "Who's asking?"

"Her daughter."

"Firstborn?"

"Only born," Amelia says.

The fox woman purses her lips. Rising halfway, she juts her chin across the room.

"Which one?" Amelia says.

The fox woman laughs. "She's your mother."

"But I don't—"

"The blonde. In the green."

The blonde in the hunter green pea coat is enormous, occupying two stools. She sits alone with her elbows planted far apart, her hands resting heavily on the table. The food on her tray remains untouched as she stares out the window at graffiti-scrawled brick. The snow is coming down fast, blown at a forty-five degree angle, almost obscuring the view.

"Sara?" Amelia says.

The blonde looks up.

"You're Sara Holbrook?"

"Why?"

"I'm your daughter." Amelia sits on the opposite stool. "I'm Amelia."

"No," the blonde says.

"You're not Sara?"

I already know the answer: she cannot be Sara. This woman, with her bad skin and greasy hair, bears no resemblance to the willowy angel gone too soon or the sculptress with the gentle soapstone curves. This woman is someone you would see on the street and not notice, or notice and feel sorry for.

Even from several feet away, I can smell the alcohol coming off her.

The blonde scoots her tray forward, sloshing soup on to her salad.

"Please," Amelia says. "Will you look at me?"

She does, and her eyes are Amelia's. They're Robert's.

Slowly, the angular features of the girl on the shrine materialize out of her swollen flesh, as if she is being sculpted right in front of us.

"I died," she says.

"That was the story," Amelia says.

"No. I'm dead and buried."

"Did he tell you it would be that way?"

Sara laughs—short, barking.

"I told *him*," she says. "He wasn't supposed to let on."

"He didn't," I say.

I hold Sara's gaze for as long as I can, but I am only a passing interest. She picks up her roll and begins tearing it apart, letting the pieces fall over her tray.

"Just like him," she says. "Ruining everything."

Amelia leans across the table and grabs Sara's wrist, stopping her movement. "You are not going to blow me off."

"Let go," Sara says.

When Amelia doesn't budge, Sara bites down on her daughter's knuckles. Amelia's hand springs open.

"You had fair warning," Sara says, and I recognize in her tone Amelia's haughtiness. I can't help smiling.

Sara picks up her tray and heads toward the kitchen.

Amelia holds out her hand for me to inspect: three red tooth marks.

"She almost drew blood," she says, but the wounds aren't that deep.

We watch as Sara hobbles toward the stairwell.

"Come on," Amelia says.

seven

IF SARA KNOWS WE are following, she does not let on. Bent against the onslaught of snow, she trudges down the street, leaving quickly-filled boot marks in her wake. At times the snow blows so hard that we lose sight of her and are forced to track her footprints as we once tracked those of deer and raccoons in the woods. Just like then, Amelia points out the unique features of the shape: the star print at the heel, the dots along the toes, the ridges in the middle. I regain some of the wonder of those missions. We are leaving human territory, entering animal realms unknown, and we must be very quiet, very careful, or everything will be lost.

Snow wets my hair and clings to my eyelashes. I no longer feel my nose. Beside me Amelia slips and slides on her high heels. Her unbalance throws me off, and soon we are grabbing at each other. She goes down on her knees, pulling me with her, but within seconds we are up again, jeans soaked, knees burning.

We trail Sara around so many corners that I begin to wonder if she does know we are here and is trying to lose us. Other footprints crowd hers, and at the next intersection, Amelia and I cannot tell Sara's boot marks apart. Amelia places her foot inside each one, but all are too big. I squint into the blowing white and, vaguely, across the street make out a hunter green form. I grab Amelia's hand and we run, dodging a cab. The driver lays on his horn; the sound reverberates in my ears long after we have left that street behind.

We come to a desolate stretch, the wind-whipped plains of Antarctica. In the distance a red neon sign flashes the word *Heart*, but this climate is inhospitable, unsuitable for civilization. The sign and its promise must be a mirage. My entire face is numb. I am afraid to look at my hands. We march on, my feet meeting the ground in sync with Amelia's. As long as she keeps going, I will keep going, but if she stops, I will fall to the ground and into a deep, deep sleep, my frozen body covered by snow, hidden until spring.

Unbelievably, *Heart* grows closer.

"Do you see?" I say, but Amelia isn't listening, she cannot hear me over the wind. She is doubled over, her eyes focused on the sidewalk. I resist the urge to put out my arm, stop her, point. I want to take a snapshot. I want to write down the story.

The unreal is becoming real.

Heart floats above us.

Soon we will pass underneath and be gone. And what will happen then? Where can we possibly go from here?

I am about to voice these questions to Amelia when a hunter green shape appears, blocking our path.

"Buy me a drink," Sara says.

To my disappointment, Heart is not a mirage or a place of dreams but an ordinary drinking establishment with low lighting, red accents, a bar along one wall, tables in the center, a stage at the back. A couple of middle-aged men sit at the bar; four young women in business attire talk intently at a table near the stage. The bartender is a young Asian man with muscular arms, wearing a tight black t-shirt. The music is electronica, dance club music, the volume kept low as a concession, I presume, for the relatively early time of day.

"Hey there, Dylan," Sara says, hefting herself onto a stool.

"You got enough cash on you for a drink?" the bartender says, but he smiles, showing two neat dimples.

"I've got my daughter on me."

"Is that a fact?" Dylan aims his dimples at us. "You're this nice lady's daughters?"

"I am," Amelia says.

"You look too young—"

"Don't give me that shit," Sara says. "Give me a Jack and Coke. And two for them."

While Amelia pays, Sara meanders through the throng of tables, considering several before choosing one in the front corner. She sits facing the window and unbuttons her coat, revealing a purple silk blouse, a row of ruffles at the neck and on the cuffs. The clothing is oddly prim, like something a much older woman wore to church and her family donated to a second hand store after her death.

"Do you always sit like that?" I ask.

Sara looks up with a pleased expression; she is still pretty, only now the viewer has to work to notice. There is something enticing in the challenge. While Amelia's beauty is difficult to dispute, displayed obtrusively on the surface, Sara's beauty must be uncovered, analyzed detail-by-detail, like a piece of modern art.

"How perceptive," she says.

I feel myself blush.

"To see what's coming?"

"I know what's coming. Snow." She tips her drink toward the window. "And more snow."

Amelia joins us. We sit in a V, Sara the focal point.

"Apparently you have a problem," Amelia says.

Sara slurps her Jack and Coke through a little red straw. "According to who?"

"Dylan."

"You're going to believe that nobody over your own mother?"

"I'm not getting you drunk," Amelia says.

Sara looks at me. "They're good, aren't they?"

I'm used to wine; in my youth I stuck to beer. Hard alcohol goes straight to my head, and soon I have a shooting pain between my eyes.

"So," Sara says, "how'd you find me?"

Amelia takes out the scrap of paper and places it in the center of the table. Sara presses the paper down with her thumb.

"That's my handwriting," Sara says.

"I found it in Robert's wallet," Amelia says, "when I was eleven."

"You call him Robert?"

"What did you call him?"

"Dad." Sara peers at the paper, then sits back, sips her drink. "Eleven? Took you a while."

"You're dead," Amelia says, putting the paper back into her pocket. "Why does it matter how long I took?"

"So what do you want now? An explanation? Fine. I was too young. I got involved with the wrong crowd."

"That's cliché."

"That's life. I was messed up. I would have been shit to you. I'm the sort who would have beaten you with coat hangers and locked you in the closet. I would have forgotten to feed you and never enrolled you in school. You think I'm kidding, but I'm not. I didn't want you. So I made myself dead. Gave us both a new start. That should have been enough."

Titling her head back, Sara downs the rest of her drink. An ice cube falls from the glass and bounces off the table.

"Buy me another," she says.

"I told you I wasn't getting you drunk."

"One drink isn't going to get me anything."

Amelia looks at me. I shrug.

"This is the last one," Amelia says and goes up to the bar.

Sara stares at me. Head-on, uninterrupted, that familiar gaze makes me want to run. I look down at my drink, wishing I'd had Amelia get me another, too.

"And who are you?" Sara says.

"Carrie. I grew up with your daughter. Your father used to tell us stories about you."

"Nothing good, I'm sure."

"No, the opposite. We idealized you."

"He always was a pretty good liar. I got that from him." She puts her hand over mine. "But it wasn't a bad childhood, was it?"

Good or bad. The choice is so simple, I almost laugh.

"A little of both," I say.

She gives my hand a satisfied pat, as if to say, I prove my point.

Amelia returns with the drink, which she places in front of Sara with unnecessary force, sloshing onto the table. "You come here every day," she says.

"Part of my routine." Sara twirls her glass, rattling the ice. "I can tell I'm letting you down all over again."

"I didn't expect my mother to be a homeless drunk."

"I have a home," Sara says. "You have the address right there on that little paper of yours."

"But you don't stay there."

"So? Why do I have to stay home just because I have one? Let my home be my cage? No. Thank. You. The walls close in, you know, if you stay in one place too long."

"You can't deny you're a drunk."

Sara's lips curl into a smug smile. "On occasion."

"No," I say. "You're more than that."

They turn their attention to me, their expressions the same—the slight cock of the head, the narrowing of the eyes. I swallow the rest of my drink.

"You're her mother," I say. "You're a woman. And we'd like to know you better."

"Why?" Sara says. "I'm not saying what you want to hear. If you're going to point blame, I'd rather you did it from a distance. I've got enough problems of my own."

"Did you think about me?" Amelia's words tumble over each other. She looks at her mother and down into her glass.

"Sorry, honey. No."

"I don't believe you."

"It's true. That life wasn't mine anymore."

Amelia runs her finger along the rim of her glass, faster and faster. All three of us watch the movement. Then she raises her hand, as if in surrender.

"How'd you do it?" she says. "How'd you die?"

"It's not hard. You just decide. You just make it so."

Sara reaches for Amelia's drink, and Amelia lets her take it.

"If you'll excuse me," Sara says when she's emptied the glass, "I

262 ✳ COURTNEY ELIZABETH MAUK

need to use the ladies'."

We watch her bulky green back sidle across the room and disappear around the corner. Amelia rests her chin on her hand and looks out the window, where the snow continues unrelentingly.

"Now we know," I say.

She swivels her chin, looks at me sidelong. "Sara's an idiot. She should never have left an address. She should have made Robert think she drove into a pond or burned in a fire. Something where there could have been no doubt."

"Is that what you're planning to do?"

Amelia blinks once and turns back to the window.

"Am I supposed to bury your body?" I say.

"No one but you knows where I am."

"The importance of personal choice," I say, "and individual impact."

"Exactly," Amelia says.

We watch the snow. The space between us is voluminous but comfortable, an unexpected sweet spot. I put my head down on the table and close my eyes.

After awhile, Amelia says, "Where is she?"

"Maybe she's sick."

"Wait here."

From behind the bar, Dylan winks at me. He has turned the music up. The businesswomen are gone; so are the two middle-aged men. In their place sits a young couple. They look like the lovers from the coffee shop, but they couldn't be. He cradles the small of her back with his hand; she rests her head on his shoulder. I wonder if, when separated, they feel the other still attached, like a phantom limb.

I need to get my phone back. I need to call Maya.

Amelia appears on the other side of the room, but she does not have Sara with her. She takes her time, stopping at the bar to talk to Dylan, who laughs at something she says. When she turns toward me, she is grinning.

"Vanished," Amelia says.

"Where?"

"Out the back door. Down the drainpipe. Who the fuck knows?"

"Shouldn't we look for her?"

"Why?" Amelia says. "She's dead, the crazy bitch." She raises her glass. "God rest my mother's dear departed soul."

✳

IF SARA IS DEAD, I have no reason to be here.

"I need to get home," I say. "I need to call my daughter."

"Not yet. We're in the middle of my mother's wake."

Amelia goes up to the bar for more drinks. I watch as she leans across the counter, flirting with Dylan. As she walks back, I watch him watch her.

"I'm too tired," I say.

"Take a little rest."

She puts her hand on the back of my head, guiding me down to the table. I stare at the condensation dripping down our glasses.

"I won't fall asleep," I say.

"Go right ahead." Amelia's fingers comb through my hair. "We have all the time in the world."

✳

WHEN I CLOSE MY eyes, I still see snow. It may never stop. We're at the dawning of a new Ice Age. The snow will continue today and tomorrow and for a hundred years, long after we're dead, our skeletons, preserved by the cold, sprawled across this table, our hair and teeth and nails intact. The snow will rise up, over the city, so that someday, when the snow melts and ice thaws, whatever species has evolved will gaze in wonder at what was buried for so long beneath their feet. They will wander through our houses, rifle through our drawers. They will hold up our toothbrushes and hair combs and say, "What is this?" and "Why is that?" They will study our photographs and try to make sense of the way our bodies moved and our minds worked, but they will come away with nothing. Only hypotheses, which are worse than lies.

They will find what remains of Amelia and me together and assume that we belonged that way. They will never know that I once had so much more.

✳

"If you could be anyone," Amelia says, "who would you be?"

I open my eyes.

Snow is falling.

"Me," I say.

"This is a game."

"I don't like games."

"Since when?"

She tells a story. Her voice is light, a shimmering thread on which the words are strung like so many jewels. Only I can't hold on to the end. The words slip into my ear and back out, falling, cracked, in a heap.

But she just keeps talking. The words come and come and never stop.

✳

I am in my car, speeding down the highway with all the windows open. Up ahead, just beyond the horizon, is California. I can tell by the way the sun's rays shoot up, out of the earth, like something rooted there, growing. Already the air is getting warmer.

If I squint into the distance, I can see Maya lying on the beach. Everything about her glows. Peter is there, too, gathering shells. He brings them to her one by one. She weighs each carefully in her hand before directing him where to place it. Together they are creating a beautiful mosaic.

I step down hard on the gas, but the horizon never seems to get any closer.

My-a. Mine.

My saving grace.

eight

THE WINDOW IS DARK; the snow has stopped.

Amelia is not across from me, but the room is full of people. They stand two deep at the bar, occupy almost every table, dance in front of the stage. A band plays rock songs from the 1950s, sped up, the singer dressed as Marilyn Monroe. With each note, she seems to swallow up the city. For a moment I become lost in her bright red lips, the perfect black O between her very white teeth.

At the bar Amelia is not within the mass of pushing shoulders and jutting elbows. When Dylan sees me, he lifts his chin toward the stage. She is there, dancing by herself in the corner. Her hips sway against the melody. She has one arm wrapped across her stomach, the other hung loose-wristed in the air.

"The moon stood still," Marilyn Monroe sings, "on Blueberry Hill."

I stand away from Amelia and watch her move. She is fluid but not graceful. Like a weed caught in the current, unaware that grace is even possible.

"Though we're apart, you're a part of me still."

Underneath the stage lights Marilyn is sweating. She wipes her forehead on the back of her hand, holding it there as if the gesture is part of the act, another flirtation with the audience. Beneath her caked makeup is the face of a man, not young.

The drummer passes Marilyn a bottle of water, but they don't break, don't even slow down. Another song begins as one song ends.

I put my hand on Amelia's shoulder. She turns and smiles.

"Dance with me," she says.

I shake my head.

She takes both my hands in hers. Our arms sway between us, but our bodies do not move.

"I need to go," I say.

She lifts her arm, twirls me underneath. We face each other, and she is just as I remember her as a little girl, messy blond hair, mischievous blue eyes. She slips something into my hand.

My cell phone. I look at the screen: the voicemail and text message icons throb.

"I have to check these," I say, but Amelia isn't listening. She is turning from me, dancing away, into the very center of the crowd.

Stepping outside is like stepping into the space between breaths.

There is no sound, no sensation but the cold, and all around, white, as yet untouched.

Snow spills over the tops of my shoes. I'm shaking, although whether from the cold or this call I don't know.

"Where are you?" Peter says.

"Chicago."

"Chicago? What are you doing there?"

"It doesn't matter."

"Why haven't you picked up your phone?"

"I'm sorry. Really. Is everything all right?"

"Everything's fine, except we've been worried about you. Glory was going to call the police tomorrow. She might already have."

"I'll call her. Where's Maya?"

"Asleep."

"What time is it?"

"Ten-thirty. Are you sure you're all right?"

"Yeah." I rub my hand across my face. "This won't happen again."

"If you need—"

"I don't. I'm okay. I'll call back in the morning."

Across the street a figure flies past on skis.

I step into the intersection, below the traffic signal. The light reflects off the snow like stained glass. I watch the colors change from red to green to yellow and back.

I begin walking.

Amelia won't look for me; she already expects me to be gone. She wrote me out of the story the moment she handed me my phone. But I would have left anyway; I was ready to go.

Up ahead I see the lights of a bus. I step to the curb, raise my arm. The bus groans to a stop, and I climb on board. "Will this get me to Harper Avenue?" I ask.

"Close enough."

I search in my purse for change, but the driver lifts his hand to stop me. I am the only passenger.

Tonight I will start driving. By noon I will be halfway to California. We'll take our time driving back. We'll stop at the Grand Canyon, buy cheap souvenirs, eat burgers and milkshakes at roadside diners, sing until our voices give out. We'll take photographs of places I have never been, and I'll put them in a scrapbook so that someday Maya will be able to look back and know that we did all this for her. She'll know what love looks like; she'll understand how it feels.

Tomorrow all of this will be memory, and soon enough, nothing at all.

Acknowledgments

I'VE HAD THE GREAT privilege of working with Victoria Barrett for two books now, and I am eternally grateful for her astute insights, sharp eye, clarity, and friendship. Thank you also to Andrew Scott. You two are literary superheroes.

Thank you to my first (and second and third)-round readers: Olena Jennings, Ryan Joe, Chandler Klang Smith, and especially David Burr Gerrard, who insisted on a present scene with Robert when I really didn't want to write one.

Gratitude to my wider community of writers, readers, teachers, and students, at Oberlin, Columbia, Juilliard, Sackett Street, *Barrelhouse*, and through the wonder of social media.

Thank you to my fellow vegans and animal rights supporters. I am grateful to everyone who, on a daily basis, makes the humane choice.

Special thanks to Mindy, Bethany, and most of all, Cil.

Thank you to my family—for the books, questions, and unwavering belief.

And thank you to my husband, Eric Wolff, whose support—in so many ways—makes this writing life of mine possible. For you, my love, always.

about the author

COURTNEY ELIZABETH MAUK is the author of the novel *Spark*. Her short work has appeared in *The Literary Review*, *PANK*, and *FiveChapters*, among others. She is an assistant editor at *Barrelhouse* and teaches at The Sackett Street Writers' Workshop and The Juilliard School. She lives in Manhattan with her husband.

Book Club Discussion Guide

1. THE DISCOVERY OF Amelia's postcard on her front door causes Carrie to spiral into the past. Why does the postcard have such a strong effect on her?

2. Orion Community is started with good intentions. Where does it go wrong? Do you think a society based on the commune's principles could be successful?

3. Discuss the characters' relationship to the setting. How is nature imagery used throughout the novel?

4. From the beginning, the power dynamic between Amelia and Carrie is unequal. Why does Carrie assume the submissive role? What does Amelia get out of their relationship? Why does their friendship remain important to them both over the decades?

5. Do you think Carrie and Peter would have separated without Amelia reentering Carrie's life?

6. How does the structure of the book reflect Carrie's psychological and emotional state?

7. Motherhood is an important part of the narrative. How do the different women (Tammy, Glory, Sara, Carrie) mother? How do their children respond?

8. How is fatherhood depicted?

9. Carrie, Amelia, Robert, and Sara are tightly intertwined. What is the significance of each to the other? Why does Sara assume such a mythic role?

10. Compare Amelia's relationship with Calvin to Carrie's relationship with Robert. Is Carrie's love for Robert purer, as she claims? What attracts the girls to these men? Why do the men respond?

11. Betrayal and sacrifice are central themes, in the novel and in Carrie's memory. Who betrays whom? Who sacrifices what for whom?

12. Repeated references are made to storytelling, imagination, and pretend play. What are the stories the characters tell each other? How does fantasy factor in?

13. Is Amelia's behavior in the present erratic? Or is she carefully plotting her actions, leading to a deliberate outcome?

14. Why does Carrie agree to go to Chicago with Amelia? What stops her from "becoming again two halves of a whole"?

15, What do you think happens to Carrie after the book ends? To Amelia?